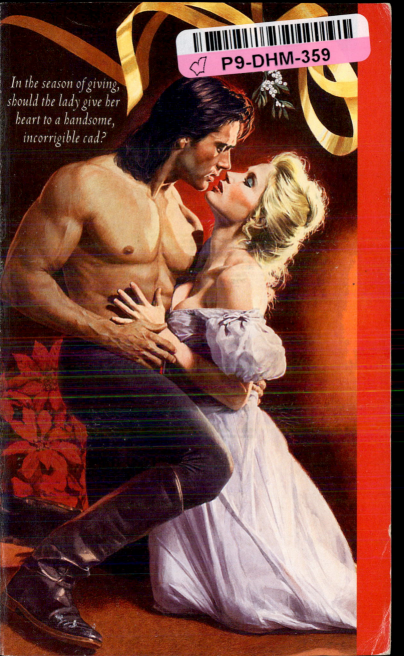

In the season of giving, should the lady give her heart to a handsome, incorrigible cad?

P9-DHM-359

Also by Johanna Lindsey

JOHANNA LINDSEY

HOME FOR THE HOLIDAYS

AVON BOOKS
An Imprint of HarperCollinsPublishers

AVON BOOKS
An Imprint of HarperCollins*Publishers*
10 East 53rd Street
New York, New York 10022-5299

Copyright © 2000 by Johanna Lindsey
Excerpts from *Heart of a Warrior* copyright © 2001 by Johanna Lindsey
ISBN: 0-380-81481-1
www.avonromance.com

First Avon Books paperback printing: November 2001
First William Morrow hardcover printing: November 2000

Avon Trademark Reg. U.S. Pat. Off. and in Other Countries, Marca Registrada, Hecho en U.S.A.
HarperCollins ® is a registered trademark of HarperCollins Publishers Inc.

Printed in the U.S.A.

10 9 8 7 6 5 4 3 2 1

They don't need ribbons nor pretty wrappings,
they need only be delivered,
a smile, a hug,
to share with someone you love.

HOME FOR *The* HOLIDAYS

Chapter 1

$\mathcal{V}$incent Everett sat in his coach across the street from the fashionable town house in London. It was one of the colder nights of the winter season, but he had slid the window open so he could see clearly across the street. He wouldn't be surprised if snow was imminent.

He wasn't sure why he was there, subjecting himself to inclement weather. He didn't doubt that his secretary, Horace Dudley, would serve the notice that gave the occupants two days to vacate the house. It wasn't that this was another stepping-stone in his decision to ruin the Ascot family, who lived there. It was more likely that he was simply bored and had had no other plans for the evening.

Even the decision to ruin this particular family wasn't an emotional one. Vincent hadn't experienced any real emotion since his childhood, nor did he ever again want to know such pain. It was much, much easier to exist with a stone for a heart, made simple matters such as evicting a family during the Christmas season just a matter of course.

No, the methodical destruction of the Ascots wasn't emotional, but it was personal. Vincent's younger brother, Albert, had made it personal, when he had put the full blame for his failed business and finances on George Ascot.

Albert had lost most of his inheritance, solely on his own. However, he had learned from his mistakes. He had taken what little was left of it and tried to start a business that would support him, so he wouldn't be a continuous drain on Vincent. And to give himself some pride. He had bought several merchant ships, opened a small office in Portsmouth. But apparently Ascot, an established shipping merchant himself, had been afraid of the competition and had set out to undermine Albert's efforts at every turn, to break him before he even began.

These were the details in Albert's letter, which was all he'd left behind before he disappeared, that and an astounding number of debts that continued to land on Vincent's door. Vincent feared that Albert had taken himself off to quietly kill himself somewhere where he wouldn't be found, as he had threatened so many times. What else was he to think, when Albert's letter had ended with "This is the only way I can think of, to no longer be an embarrassment or burden to you"?

Albert's demise had left Vincent without family, though to be honest, he'd never really felt a part of his own family, so his lack of one now hardly made a difference to him. His parents had died just after Vincent reached his majority, within a year of each other, leaving only the two brothers. With no other relatives, even distant ones, the brothers should have been close. Not so. Albert might have felt a closeness, or more to the point, a dependency, but then Albert expected the world and everything in it to revolve around him, a silly notion that their parents had fostered by making him their joy, their amusement, their favorite. Vincent had merely been the reserved, boring heir they never took notice of.

It was amazing that Vincent had never hated his brother, but then you had to experience emotion to hate. By the same token, there had been no love, either, for his weakling of a brother, merely a tolerance because he was "family." That he had picked up the gauntlet, as it were, on Albert's behalf was more a long-standing habit, as well as a matter of pride. It was a blight on his own name, that George Ascot had successfully crushed an Everett without consequences. He would soon know differently. It was the last thing that Vincent could do for Albert, to at least pay back Ascot in kind.

The snow he had been expecting arrived, just as the door opened across the street to Dudley's knock. Vincent's view was hampered by the white flakes, but he could still make out a flowing skirt, so a female had answered the knock. Ascot himself wouldn't be there. Reports were that he had set sail on one of his ships in the first week of September, and more than three months later, had yet to return to England. His absence was making this retaliation simple. When Ascot did return, he would find his credit canceled with many of his

6

merchant suppliers, and his home lost to him due to lack of payment on demand.

Vincent hadn't decided yet whether to continue his campaign after tonight or to wait for Ascot's return. Tonight's eviction would be a decisive blow, the culmination of several weeks' work, but hardly satisfactory when Ascot wouldn't be there to know of it yet.

Actually, this whole matter of revenge was rather distasteful. It wasn't something he wanted to do, had ever done before, or likely ever would again, but was something he felt he *had* to do this one time. So he would as soon get it over and done with. But Ascot wasn't obliging in that, being out of the country for longer than expected.

He should have returned by now. Vincent had counted on his being back by now. Waiting was not something he did well. And waiting in his coach, in the cold, when he didn't need to be there and still wasn't even sure why he was there, was starting to annoy him, especially since Dudley was taking his sweet time delivering the notice. How bloody long did it take to hand over a piece of paper?

Across the street, the door finally closed. But Vincent's secretary still stood there facing it, unmoving. Had he accomplished his task, or had the door been closed on him before he could? What the devil was he doing, standing there in the snow doing nothing?

Vincent was about to leave the coach himself to find out what was going on, when Dudley finally turned about and headed back toward him. Vincent opened the coach door, more in his impatience than to get Dudley out of the biting cold sooner. But Dudley didn't rush inside when he got there, he didn't enter the coach at all, was once again just standing there in the snow, as if he'd gone totally daft.

However, before Vincent could ask about this strange behavior, Dudley announced, "I have never in my life done anything so despicable, my lord, nor will I ever do so again. I quit."

Vincent raised a questioning brow at him. "Quit as in—?"

"You will have my formal resignation on your desk in the morning."

Vincent savored a moment of amazement. It wasn't often that he could be so thoroughly surprised. But then his impatience returned.

"Get in the bloody coach, Mr. Dudley. You can

explain yourself when we are out of this damnable weather."

"No, sir," Dudley replied stiffly. "I will find my own way home, thank you very much."

"Don't be absurd. You won't find a hack this time of night."

"I will manage."

With that, the secretary closed the coach door and started marching down the street. Ordinarily Vincent would have shrugged and dismissed the man from his mind, but he was in an impatient frame of mind, which was as close as he came to being emotional.

He found himself leaving the coach himself and marching after Dudley to demand, "What the devil happened at that house to give you leave of your senses?"

Horace Dudley swung around, his face suffused with emotional color rather than paled from the cold. "If I must have further discourse with you, my lord, I fear I will disgrace myself beyond regret. Please, simply accept my resignation and leave it go at—"

"The devil I will. You've been with me for eight years. You do not just resign over a small matter—"

"Small!?" the little man burst out. "If you could have seen the stricken look on that poor girl's face, it would have broken your heart as it did mine. And such a pretty girl. Her face is going to haunt me the rest of my days."

Having said so and apparently believing it, Dudley scurried off down the street once more, refusing to speak more of it. Vincent let him go this time and turned a scowl on the house in question.

The property belonged to him now. He'd called in a considerable number of favors to coerce the previous owner to ignore his verbal commitment with George Ascot and sell him the deed instead. Ascot had had a gentlemen's agreement with that previous owner, had paid him a very large portion down on the town house and agreed to pay off the balance within a few years. There still being a mortgage, he was not yet in possession of the deed.

Vincent had bought the deed and sent a demand for the balance from Ascot to be paid immediately. He was well aware that Ascot wasn't in the country to receive the demand or arrange to borrow elsewhere to pay it, thus he would lose the house and everything he had put into it—and only find out about it upon his return, when it was too late to salvage his investment.

It had been a well-aimed blow at Ascot's finances, as well as his reputation, since it wouldn't go over well with his creditors that he had been evicted from his residence. Vincent certainly hadn't expected to lose his valuable secretary over the matter, though.

A pretty girl, eh? She must be the daughter. No other female in that house would be so affected by the eviction, to wear a "stricken" look, since Ascot only had one female in his family, a daughter who had just reached marriageable age. His wife had passed on years ago. There was also a young son.

Vincent found himself approaching the door to the house, just out of curiosity, he assured himself. But after knocking and waiting several long minutes, with snow continuing to collect on the shoulders of his greatcoat, he concluded that curiosity was a silly thing by all accounts, and his own didn't need to be satisfied.

He turned to leave. The door opened. Pretty? The girl standing there haloed in the soft light behind her took his breath away. This was who he had evicted into the snow-covered streets? This exquisitely beautiful, forlorn creature? Bloody hell.

Chapter 2

$\mathcal{L}$arissa Ascot stood in the open doorway staring at the large form before her, but she wasn't really seeing anything. Snow was blowing in her face, but she didn't really notice that either, or even feel the cold.

It was too much, all at once, much too much to deal with on top of everything else that had been visited upon her in the last few weeks. The butcher, as well as the baker, both denying her further credit until the current accounts were settled. Her brother, Thomas, sickening and needing constant attendance. Her father's banker apologizing, but patiently explaining why she couldn't have access to her father's funds without his permission. Watching the household funds, which had been ample and should have lasted nearly a year for incidentals, dwindle down to nothing because she had been forced not only to settle with those nasty merchants who had shown up at her door demanding immediate payment on outstanding debts, but also to pay cash just to put a bit of food on the table.

Most of her servants had already been let go, an event that had made her literally sick to her stomach in the doing. Many of those servants had been with her family for years, had made the move with them from Portsmouth to London three years ago when her father had expanded his business and relocated there. It had been horrible for them to lose their jobs during the holiday season, but just as traumatic for her to have to be the one to tell them. But she had been unable to pay them this month, and with her father already a month late in returning, she could no longer assure them that he would be home soon to settle with them.

And now this . . . this eviction. Unexpected, completely without warning. The little man had said a demand had been sent by the new owner through the posts, that there had been ample warning, but she didn't read her father's mail, so she hadn't seen it. New owner? How could Mr. Adams, whom they had bought the house from, sell it out from under them? Was that legal? When there was only a few thousand pounds remaining before the house was completely theirs?

She couldn't comprehend why all this was happening, why merchants they had dealt with for several years now no longer trusted her family to settle with them at the end of the year as was their custom, why they had lost their home. One day to leave. They were to vacate by tomorrow, pack up everything and be gone. How? She didn't have any money left to hire wagons to move them. And to where? Their old home in Portsmouth had been sold. They had no other relatives. The old family estate near Kent was merely a property, uninhabitable, and besides, the doctor had warned that if Thomas didn't remain in bed and out of drafts, he wouldn't recover, could even take a turn for the worse.

"Are you all right, miss?"

The body standing before her slowly took shape, a tall man in a greatcoat that was deceiving of form; skinny, fat, it was hard to tell in one of those coats, not that it mattered. Larissa was merely trying to focus on *something* that might draw her out of the mire her mind was still in. Somewhat handsome, though that was hard to really discern when his cheeks and long nose were covered with snow. Not too young, perhaps nearing thirty . . .

"Miss?"

The question? Ah, was she all right? If she began to laugh hysterically, would he still wonder?

"No, I don't believe so," she said honestly, though she realized she'd just opened the door on further conversation that she didn't want, so she added quickly, "If you're here to see my father, he isn't home."

"I know." At her frown, he continued, "I'm Vincent Everett, Baron Everett of Windsmoor."

"Baron of— You're the new owner?"

Incredible. Such gall, for him to show up after his devastating blow had already been delivered. Was he there to gloat, then? Or merely to make sure that they would comply with the eviction so he wouldn't have to send round the magistrate to physically oust them? Which was going to be the case anyway. There was simply no way that she could get everything they owned out of the house by tomorrow, even if she had someplace to move to.

She supposed the furnishings could be stored at her father's office on the docks. She and Thomas might even have been able to sleep there temporarily—if her brother weren't so sick. But that office was drafty even in the summer. To subject Thomas to the cold that floated up from the Thames was unthinkable. Yet what other choice did she have? There was no money left for lodgings, no money left for food. She had put off selling their possessions, hoping with each day's passing that that would be the day her father would return and make everything right again. But she'd put it off too long. Now there was no time left . . .

Her instinct was to close the door on the baron. He might own the house now, but she was still in possession of it—for one more day. But he hadn't said why he was there yet. And just because her world was falling apart didn't mean she had to abandon common courtesies. She could give him at least five more seconds to state his business, *then* she would close the door on him.

"Why are you here, Lord Everett?"

"My secretary was rather upset."

"The man here before you?"

"Yes. And from what he said, I'm beginning to think a—misunderstanding may have occurred."

"Misunderstanding? I have a letter of eviction. It's quite clear, actually, and if it weren't, your secretary read it aloud so I couldn't possibly—misunderstand."

She heard the bitterness in her tone, found it appalling that she could so reveal herself to a complete stranger, but couldn't manage to contain such overwhelming emotion. Better a bit of anger, though, than tears. The tears would come, would have arrived already if she hadn't been so dazed by this last and worst shock, but hopefully she could hold them back until she was alone.

"I did not say 'mistake,' miss," he corrected her. "I was referring to something else, which cannot be cleared up until your father's return. So I will need an address where you can be reached after tomorrow."

The fight went out of her, leaving her shoulders drooping. Had she really thought, just for the barest moment, that his "misunderstanding" might mean they wouldn't lose the house after all?

"I don't have an address to give you," she replied in a near whisper. "I truly have no idea where we will be after tomorrow."

"A quite unacceptable answer," he said with some impatience in his tone. He then reached into a coat pocket and handed her a card. "You may stay at this address until your father makes other arrangements for you. I will send my coach in the morning to assist you."

"Can we not just . . . stay here . . . until this matter you've mentioned is settled?"

There was the barest hesitation before he replied succinctly and emphatically, "No."

She'd had to force that last question out of her. It went completely against the grain for her to have to ask, beg as it were, for anything, and in particular, from a stranger. But if he was going to supply lodging as his card indicated, why could he not supply this lodging? had been her desperate thought. But a foolish thought, obviously.

And his "no" was the catalyst that sent him on his way, a dark shadow quickly fading to nothing in the swirling snow.

It was another moment or so before Larissa thought to close the door and did so. She even managed to take herself upstairs to check on Thomas. He was sleeping fitfully, the fever that visited him each night still lingering.

Mara sat beside his bed, sleeping in the comfortable chair drawn there. Mara Sims had been Thomas's nanny, and Larissa's as well. In fact, she had been with them as long as Larissa could remember. She had refused to abandon them just because her wage was a bit tardy, as she put it. Her sister, Mary, had likewise refused to leave.

Mary used to be their housekeeper, but when they'd lost their cook back in Portsmouth, she'd admitted that she much preferred the kitchen domain and had taken a downgrade in position to do what she loved best. The haughty housekeeper who had replaced her had been the first to quit right after the creditors began showing up at the door. Amazing how the news of their financial difficulty had spread through the neighborhood so fast.

They would have a roof over their heads . . .

Larissa should have been experiencing some relief about the new lodgings, the biggest worry out of the way, temporarily at least. But as she went to her room and began the miserable chore of packing her personal belongings, she couldn't quite grasp the relief she should be feeling.

Nor had any gratitude shown up yet where the baron was concerned. His offer of alternate lodging had been for his convenience, not theirs. It wasn't help in the traditional sense, was simply that *he* wanted to keep track of them for his own purpose, whatever that was. The "misunderstanding" apparently wasn't anything drastic that might alter their changed circumstances.

She was probably still too dazed by it all to feel much of anything just yet. Which was just as well. At least she wouldn't be crying all night long while she packed. And the tears actually held off until the wee hours, when she went to sleep with them on her cheeks.

Chapter 3

$\mathcal{V}$incent stood before the fireplace in his bedroom, a snifter of warmed brandy in hand. He was staring at the dancing flames as if mesmerized, yet he wasn't actually seeing the fire. It was a piquant face that he saw, framed with burnished gold locks and eyes that were neither green or blue, but a light blending of both colors in a unique shade of turquoise he'd never seen before.

He never should have gone to have a look at Larissa Ascot. He never should have got anywhere near her. She should have remained faceless, merely "Ascot's daughter," an indirect casualty in his small war. But having seen her, the decision to seduce her had been the easiest decision yet in his campaign against the Ascots. Ruin her for marriage, another blow against the family's good name. That had been his thought when he had handed her his card. On reflection, though, he knew it was just an excuse, and a paltry one at that.

It had been a long time since he had wanted something, really wanted something, for himself. He wanted her. Revenge gave him all the excuse he needed to have her, would ease his conscience—if he had one. He wasn't sure if he had one or not. The lack of emotion in his life included guilt, so it was hard to tell.

The next day he was in the entry hall to greet her when she arrived at his home. Her surprise was evident.

"I thought the address you gave me would be for another property of yours that you let out, one that was presently vacant. If I had known you were offering the hospitality of your own home, I would have . . ."

"Declined?" he supplied with interest when she failed to finish. "Would you really?"

She blushed profusely. "I would have liked to."

"Ah." He smiled at her. "But we can't always do as we like."

No indeed, or he would carry her straight away to his bed. She was even more beautiful than he recalled, or perhaps it was merely the bright daylight in the hall that revealed more of her perfection. Petite, narrow of waist, finely garbed in a fur-trimmed coat over mauve velvet skirts. A small, narrow nose. Dark gold brows, more a slash than an arch. Unblemished skin except for a small mole on the corner of her chin. Tiny earlobes with teardrop pearls hanging from them. She was every inch a lady, merely lacking a title that said so.

The Ascots had not been poor, likely were still well off. They were gentry. There was even an earl somewhere in their ancestry. They were quite socially acceptable to the *ton*, even though George had gone into business, which was not so frowned upon these days as it used to be. Albert had tried to do the same . . .

The only reason that Vincent had found it so easy to ruin Ascot's financial reputation was that he was not in the country at the moment to put an end to the rumors that had spread about his dire straits. His prolonged absence had set his creditors to panic.

She came with an entourage, two women in their late fifties who looked nearly identical, and a pile of blankets that his coachman had carried in for them.

"We have bedding," Vincent thought to point out.

Larissa was still blushing over being there. Her blush brightened more as she explained, "That's my brother, Thomas. He has a dreadful cold. He wanted to walk, but the illness has sapped his strength."

The blankets wiggled. The son was sick? Why had none of the reports he had on the family mentioned that? Vincent was pricked by his elusive conscience, but only for a moment. He nodded at his housekeeper, who had been apprised of the impending guests. She in turn nodded at the coachman to follow her. The two elderly servants did as well.

They were alone for the moment, there in the wide entry hall. Vincent wasn't sure how to proceed. He was used to dealing with women in a straightforward manner. His title and wealth had always opened more doors for him than not, and the "nots" simply weren't worth the effort. So he had never actually resorted to a planned seduction before. And the few that had been planned against him all seemed to include food in the agenda for some reason beyond his comprehension, as if women naturally assumed that a man without a wife must be starving, when any man of his position would have a perfectly good cook on staff, which he did.

However, the thought of food reminded him, "You are in time for luncheon."

"No, thank you, Lord Everett, I couldn't possible intrude," she replied.

"Intrude on what?"

"Your family."

"I have no family. I live alone here."

It was a simple statement of fact, not meant to elicit sympathy from her. Yet he didn't mistake the brief show of it that crossed her face before she recollected that she was in the enemy's camp, so to speak.

Her attitude was understandable. She was not bubbling over with gratitude for his assistance, just the opposite. Her stiffness, her reticence, both spoke volumes. She no doubt saw him as the enemy, whether she was really aware that he was one or not. He'd put her out of her home. That alone would bring dislike, possibly even hate. Which was why the show of sympathy was so interesting. She had to have quite a compassionate nature to feel sympathy, however brief, for someone she likely despised at the moment.

She had given a paltry excuse to decline eating with him, and having disposed of it, he wasn't going to give her another opportunity to refuse a simple meal, especially when it was such a perfect opportunity for them to become better acquainted. He took her arm and led her to the dining room, sat her down and moved away from her to put her at ease. He'd noticed her nervousness as well as her shyness, or rather, her disinclination to look at him directly, and in his experience, there was only one reason for that . . .

It was fairly obvious that despite any resentment toward him that she might be harboring, she was still attracted to him.

It was not unexpected. Women of all ages were drawn not only to his looks, but to the challenge he represented. They wanted to crack his shell. They couldn't grasp the fact that cracking it would gain them nothing, since he had nothing inside it to offer.

As for Larissa, he would have to take full advantage of her attraction to him, to get around her present dislike. And perhaps use her sympathy to his advantage as well. Actually, he decided that anything would be permissible in this seduction. He would be absolutely ruthless about it if he had to be. For once, having a lack of emotion and conscience was going to be quite beneficial.

He took the seat across from her and gave a nod to the waiting servants to begin the meal. It wasn't until the first course was over that she noticed that he was staring at her in a sensual manner. Her blush was immediate when she did notice. He did not stop.

Vincent had been told on numerous occasions, in numerous ways, that his eyes revealed his emotions. Which was quite amusing to him since these occasions were usually during sexual interludes and his passions were tepid at best. It was the color of his eyes that gave the impression, he supposed, of more desire than was actually present. Amber jewels, molten gold, devilishly wicked, sexy, he'd heard it all and discounted it all. His eyes were merely a very light shade of brown with a few gold flecks, nothing extraordinary, in his opinion. Of course, living with them for twenty-nine years made them quite ordinary to him.

But if Larissa imagined heated desire in them when he was only admiring her beauty over the entrée, well, that was to his good. He would much prefer to not have to spell it out, this seduction, if she was too dense to realize he was seducing her. And it wasn't as if she could run off and hide from it, when she had nowhere to run to. He needed only assure her that the choice would be hers to make, and he would do that at an appropriate time. Less than an hour after her arrival was definitely too soon.

Still—he didn't stop staring. He knew he should. He simply couldn't.

He found it incredible that Ascot had managed to hide this exquisite daughter of his from the *ton*, to keep her under wraps, as it were. This was their third year in London. Surely someone of note would have discovered her by now, particularly since the family had lived in one of the more desirable neighborhoods, well populated with titles. Yet she wasn't engaged nor being courted, and her name had never reached the gossip mills. This would have been her come-out Season—if her father had been home to "bring her out."

He decided to ask, "Why is it you're unknown to society here?"

"Perhaps because I've made no effort to be known," she replied with a light shrug.

"Why not?"

"I didn't want to move to London. I grew up in Portsmouth, was perfectly happy there. I hated my father for bringing us to London. And for the first year we were here, I behaved like the foolish child I was and tried every way I could to make my father regret the move. I was an utter brat. I spent the next year trying to make it up to him, to make our home here a real home. Meeting my neighbors wasn't part of either agenda . . . My God, why did I just tell you all of that?"

Vincent burst out laughing, wondering the same thing. And she looked so surprised—at herself. That was what he found most amusing, that he disturbed her enough to cause her to forget standard protocol.

"Nervous chatter, I would imagine," he supplied helpfully, still smiling.

"I'm not nervous," she denied, but she looked down as she said it, still shying away from his direct stares, which he had no intention of stopping.

"It's normal to be nervous. We are not well acquainted—yet."

"Well acquainted" implied many things, and she apparently objected to all of them. "Nor will we ever be," she retorted stiffly, then thought to add, "I know why I am here."

"You do?" he asked with interest.

"Certainly. It was the only way that you could be assured another meeting with my father when he returns, to straighten out this mysterious misunderstanding of yours—which you refuse to explain."

A pointed reminder that he was not being completely truthful with her, which he in turn pointedly ignored, since he had no intention of revealing his real motives. Revenge worked best when it struck in surprise, after all. But he did want to know just how much of an upper hand he held at the moment, where she was concerned, since she was now a prime piece in the equation.

He had made assumptions, when she had confessed she didn't know where her family would be moving to. He had pictured her destitute and living on the streets. But those earbobs she was wearing said otherwise. Yet he wanted her to have no other recourse than to remain right where she was. The last thing he wanted was for her to be able to up and leave his house once she realized he was going to make every effort to get her into his bed.

It made the difference between a speedy, straightforward campaign for him, and a long, tedious one during which he would have to be careful of every word he said to her. And time *was* of the essence, since her father could return at any moment to rescue her from ruination.

It wouldn't be too difficult, however, to assure that she was destitute, or at least to have her think so, and to that end he said, "If you have any valuable jewelry, you can lock it in my safe while you are here. My servants are trustworthy, or most of them are, but we have a couple new maids that haven't proven themselves yet."

"I do have a few nice pieces, from my mother. They would have been sold only as a last resort. There are paintings, however, that I should have sold already. I prevaricated too long, thinking my father would return sooner. I should see to their disposal tomorrow."

"Nonsense. You've no need to sell off your belongings now. You can wait here for your father. He will rectify everything when he returns, I'm sure."

"I'm sure as well, but I don't like being without any money whatsoever, and I really did go through the last of our funds for Thomas's medicine. He will also need more . . ."

"Your furniture is being stored as we speak. I repeat, there is no reason for you to dispose of it. My personal physician is also due this week, to examine my staff—something I arrange for each year at this time—so feel free to use his services for your brother while he is here. But how is it possible that you are completely without funds? Is George Ascot that inconsiderate that—"

"Certainly not!" she cut in indignantly. "But our creditors heard some ridiculous rumor that he wouldn't be returning and demanded I clear their accounts. And not just one, but all of them showed up at our door. They wouldn't believe me that he would soon be home. I was forced to deplete my household funds to satisfy them. And then Thomas caught that horrid cold that got worse and worse until I feared . . ."

She broke off, overcome with emotion.

Strangely, Vincent found himself wanting to put his arms around her to comfort her. Good God, what an absurd thought—for him. He shoved the inclination aside. He was making progress, in getting her to talk. He wasn't going to muck that up with some silly urge to fix everything for her, when her plight was all his doing in the first place.

"And then I added to your woes." He managed to feign a convincing sigh.

She nodded, in complete agreement. She was also back to not looking at him. No matter. He *had* made progress. She had opened up, and easily. But then she seemed to have a wide range of easily pricked emotions, and it was not difficult at all to manipulate emotions if you knew which cords to yank on. He was learning hers.

"I still don't understand why you bought our house, or how you bought it for that matter, when it was already sold to us," she remarked.

"Simple business, Miss Ascot. I acquired the deed from the possessor of the deed. It's what I do, buy and sell, invest, supply what is in demand at opportune times to reap huge profits. Be it a certain style of architecture, a piece of art, or whatever, when I hear that someone is looking for something in particular, I make an effort to supply it, if it's within my means and inclination to do so."

"You're saying you have a buyer for our house already, that that's why you purchased it out from under us?"

"My dear girl, your father was given the opportunity to pay the remainder of his debt to complete his own purchase. Had he done so, the deed would have been his."

"But then you would have purchased the house for nothing, would have seen no profit on it."

"True, but that is a chance I take in what I do. I either reap excessive rewards, or I break even. Occasionally I even take a loss, but not enough for it to have kept me from becoming quite rich in my endeavors."

"That implies you have made your own fortune," she concluded.

"Indeed."

"No grand inheritance, then, when you gained your title?" she asked next.

It was easy to see that she was trying to discomfit him, and perhaps catch him in a lie. She wasn't very adept at table-turning, though.

He was amused by the effort. He didn't even

mind sharing a few particulars of his life with her. Actually, he supposed he was a prime candidate for extreme sympathy, if all the facts of his life were taken into account. Not that he would ever reveal all those facts, but a few to work on her sympathies certainly wouldn't hurt.

"My title came with the entailed family estate in Lincolnshire, which I refuse to ever step foot on again, since it holds nothing but bad memories for me. The rest of the family wealth, mediocre as it was, was left to my favored younger brother, now deceased."

He said it without inflection, yet the frown lines came immediately to her brow. She really was too compassionate for her own good. It was going to be her downfall—where he was concerned.

Uncomfortably she announced, "I'm sorry, I didn't mean to pry."

"Of course you did. It's human nature to pry."

"But polite to refrain," she insisted, determined to be at fault for the moment.

"Stop chastising yourself, Larissa. Politeness is not required of you here."

"On the contrary, politeness is mandatory at all times," she countered.

He smiled. "Is this a reminder for yourself, or do you really believe that? And before you answer, take note that I have just dismissed formalities between us in the use of your first name. You are invited to do the same. Keep in mind also that people are allowed their moments of impoliteness, when warranted, especially between close acquaintances."

Her blush was back in full bloom. So was her stiff tone as she stood up to say, "We are barely acquainted, nor will I be here long enough for that to change. I will in fact make an effort to be as unobtrusive as possible while in your house. Now if you will excuse me, *Lord Everett*, I must check on my brother."

He sat back with his wineglass in hand, which he swirled once before finishing off. She wanted formality between them, had just stressed it. He wondered how her formality, and her politeness for that matter, would hold up once he had her naked body snuggled next to him in bed. Not very well, he hoped.

Chapter 4

*T*homas was settled in and letting Mara spoon-feed him. He didn't like being treated like a baby. He truly hated it. But during the worst of his fever when he had insisted on feeding himself, he had never finished his meals because he was simply too weak.

Having caught him in the stubborn lie that he wasn't hungry, merely because he was too tired to finish on his own, Larissa no longer gave him the choice. He'd be fed or he'd be fed, and those were the only options he had until he was completely well again.

The room that he had been put in was much larger than his room at home. So was the bed. He seemed so small in it. But then he was small for his age, both skinnier and shorter than other boys of ten. Their father, a tall man himself, had assured him that he would catch up soon enough, that he hadn't sprouted himself until he was twelve.

Thomas might be behind other boys his age in height, but he was far superior in intelligence. If he weren't so stubborn at times, and prone to a temper tantrum on occasion, Larissa would swear there was a full-grown man inside that little body. His keen observations were often just too adultlike. But his boundless energy, when he wasn't sick, was a firm reminder that he was still a child.

His energy, or current lack of it, contributed to his being a really rotten patient, full of complaints. He didn't like staying in bed, and hated the weakness that had come upon him since the onset of the fevers.

As she approached the bed, Thomas wouldn't look up at her, still pouting over the move, as if there had been some way she could have prevented it. She wished she'd had the luxury to do a little pouting of her own, but all she'd been able to do was cry.

She tried to sound cheerful, however, when she asked, "No chills from that cold ride here?"

"Cold? You had me so buried in those blankets, Lari, I roasted."

"Good, roasting is fine as long as you didn't catch a chill."

Mara tried to hide a smile, unsuccessfully. Thomas glared at them both. Larissa "tsked."

Thomas called her Lari only when he was annoyed with her, because he hoped it would annoy her as well, it sounding like a man's name. When all was right with his world, he called her Rissa, as their father did.

"Why did we have to come here?" Thomas brought his real complaint out in the open—once again. "This room is like a hotel room."

"And how would you know what a hotel room looks like?" Larissa countered.

"I went with Papa once, to meet that French wine merchant at his hotel."

"Oh, well, yes, this house is much bigger than ours, and it does seem very—impersonal, from

47

what I've seen of it so far, like a hotel. Baron Windsmoor has no family, though, which I suppose accounts for that."

"We won't have to stay here long, will we?"

"Not long a'tall," she assured him. "Just as soon as father returns—"

"You've been saying that for weeks now. When is he going to return?"

It was hard to remain cheerful when Thomas was asking the very things that she had been asking herself—and had run out of answers for. Two months was all he was to be gone, which would have allowed a week, two at the most, to conduct his business. He had promised to be home by the beginning of November. It was now a full month beyond that. Bad weather might be responsible for some delay, but four weeks worth?

No, she could no longer hide from the fact that something must have gone terribly wrong on his journey. Ships were lost at sea all the time, with no one ever really knowing what had happened. There were even pirates rumored to still roam the very waters that their father would have sailed through, ready to pounce on a heavily laden merchantman. She'd had time and plenty to imagine the worst, shipwrecked, stranded on a deserted island, starving . . .

Her worry had become so intense it now seemed a part of her. She wanted desperately to share it with someone, needed a shoulder to cry on, but she had to do without either. She had to be strong for Thomas's sake, to continue to assure him that everything would be all right, when she no longer believed that it would.

To that end she said, "The best-laid plans don't always lie down right, Tommy. Father hoped to secure a new market in New Providence, but what if there was none there? He would have had to sail to the next island then, wouldn't he? And if there was nothing there, either?"

"But why did he have to sail so far when he could have found a new market closer to home?"

She gave her brother a stern look. "Haven't we discussed this before, and several times? Weren't you listening to me the last time?"

"I always listen to you," he grumbled. "You just don't always make sense."

She didn't take him to task for that, knew very well that he was merely being defensive because his illness was making him forgetful. He'd either been half-asleep during most of their recent conversations, or his fever had been raging, so it was no wonder he couldn't remember them all.

"Well, let's see if we can both make sense out of what happened, because I still don't understand it all either," she told him, hoping that would make him feel better. "Most companies in the same line of business enjoy some friendly or even not so friendly competition. That's the nature of business, you'll agree?" She waited a moment. He nodded. She continued, "But when one bad apple gets into the pot, it can ruin the whole pot."

"Can you stick to specifics please?"

She "tsked," but did. "That new shipping line that opened late last summer, The Winds line, I believe it was called, was a welcome addition to a thriving market—until they proved to be completely underhanded. Instead of seeking their own markets, they set about stealing those already in good hands."

"Father's?"

"Not just Father's, though they did seem to single him out the most. He never told me about it himself. He wouldn't, not wanting to worry me. What I know, I overheard when his captains or clerk came to the house. Apparently The Winds was trying to put him completely out of business, *and* nearly succeeded. I'd never seen him so furious as he was those last few weeks before he left, after all but one of his ships returned to port without their scheduled cargoes, because The Winds captains had followed his and overpaid in each port."

"Even that nice French wine—?"

"Yes," she cut in, trying to keep him from talking so much, since that seemed to wear him out, too. "Even he ignored the contract Father had with him to sell to the higher-bidding captain."

"But what good is a contract if it can be so easily broken?"

"From what I heard, they weren't exactly broken, just some flimsy excuses given as to why the merchandise wouldn't be forthcoming. The nature of business, I suppose," Larissa said with a shrug she wasn't really feeling, adding, "It's hard to fault the merchants when they had the chance to reap huge, unexpected profits."

"I don't find it hard to fault them a'tall," he disagreed. "Contracts are made for good reason, so the market can be dependable."

She should have known better than to fluff it

off, when Thomas was being groomed, even at his young age, to take over their father's company someday. "Be that as it may, this happened all across Europe. The Winds ships showed up in every port that ours did. Rather easy to conclude that it was deliberate, that they were specifically following our line to obtain *our* cargoes. And *that's* why Father sailed so far from home. He couldn't compete with The Winds, which was paying unheard-of prices, or he would have made no profit on the cargoes."

Thomas frowned. "I think this is where I don't understand. How was that other shipping company going to make any profit if it was paying so high for its cargoes?"

"They weren't. They apparently had money to throw away on this particular tactic. Secure the market first, then worry about getting the prices back to reasonable later. It was merely a ploy, and one that worked. Father couldn't risk sending his ships back to the same merchants, only to have the same thing happen again, so in that, The Winds line won; they now have those old markets."

"Do you think Papa was able to find new markets, then?" Thomas asked.

"Certainly," she said, trying to sound confident. "And he had planned to expand to the West Indies eventually. So this may turn out to be a very good move in the end."

"Though forced on him before he was ready."

Often she wished Thomas weren't so smart and would just accept an explanation when given as most children did at his age, rather than question and point out all the flaws in her logic. "Would you like me to tell you what I think?"

"Do I have a choice?"

She smiled. "No, you don't. I think this is going to turn out very well in the end. I doubt The Winds line will survive very long, and when they go under, Father will be able to get back his old contacts, and with the new ones he gains from this trip, why, he'll probably have to buy new ships to keep up with it all."

"And *I* think you're just hoping The Winds will go under, when they aren't likely to, if they had such deep pockets to begin with, to get away with what they did."

"Oh, I'm not talking about their finances. I'm talking about the bad will they've spread, starting out in such an unethical manner. Consider, the merchants who sold to them for the huge profits know exactly what they were up to, and anyone that underhanded can't be trusted. But many of the goods involved are perishable, in need of timely delivery—and trustworthy captains to arrive on time. If The Winds line is late in the future, the cargoes could spoil before they are even picked up, and of course, they won't be bought spoiled. Do you see what I mean?"

"So you're thinking that Father's old contacts will want to deal with him again, because he's well established and, of course, trustworthy?"

"I think they will prefer to, yes . . . and will you look what we've done. We've put Mara to sleep with all this talk of business that she doesn't find the least bit interesting. But no wonder, it's time for your nap as well."

"I'm not tired," he complained.

"I saw those eyes drooping."

"Didn't," he grumbled.

"Did, too. And besides, you need the rest whether you sleep or not. When your fever is completely gone, then we can negotiate an end to these naps."

He conceded. He loved to negotiate, which was why she'd mentioned it.

She headed to the door. But he stopped her there with one last question that she really wasn't prepared for.

"Where are we going to put the Christmas tree this year, Rissa?"

It wasn't the question, but the quaver she heard in his little voice as he asked it. It was her undoing. She hadn't even thought about spending Christmas without her father. She hadn't thought that far ahead, couldn't, because there was too much grief awaiting her down that road.

"It's too soon to think of the tree, this early in the month. But we'll have one, Tommy, even if we have to share the Baron's—"

"I don't want to share, I want to put on the decorations we've made. You did bring them with us, didn't you?"

No, she hadn't. They'd been stored in the attic and had gone with the other furnishings to wherever Lord Everett had had them taken.

"They'll be here when it's time," was the best she could offer him at the moment. "So please don't worry about it. Just get better, so you'll be able to do some of the decorating yourself."

She had to get out of there. Tears were already

streaming down her cheeks, which she didn't want him to see. It wasn't going to be a normal Christmas for them this year. She was afraid, so very afraid that they would be spending it without their father.

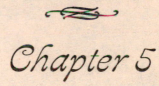

Chapter 5

$\mathcal{L}$arissa wasn't sure how she found the bedroom that she had been given, when she could barely see through her tears, and no one had answered any of the knocking she had done on all the doors between hers and Thomas's, so she'd had to peek into each room. But she finally did spot her trunks piled at the foot of the bed in one of the last two rooms at the very end of the hall, a much longer distance from her brother than she cared for.

Had she thought Thomas's room was immense compared to his old one? The one she had been given was even grander. There was even a separate dressing room attached to it, with a large bathroom off of that, and another connecting door led to still another bedroom, which, to her shock, she realized was the baron's bedroom. She'd been put in the lady's half of the master bedroom suites. Good heavens, why? Surely a house this size had other rooms for guests, and hadn't she just passed at least a half dozen in the hall?

This wouldn't do, must be a mistake, and she would have to tell the housekeeper—just as soon as she could manage to stop crying. To accomplish that, she sat down on the edge of the bed and gave in to all the emotions that were crowding in on her. Oddly enough, a few of those emotions were new to her and took over, drying up the well.

She had let Thomas distract her, purposely, since she knew he could. It was why she had raced to his room. But she was alone now, her thoughts once again disturbed by that strange luncheon she had shared with the baron.

She didn't know what to make of him, but he had flustered her beyond anything she had ever experienced. It wasn't that he was so very handsome that he had taken her breath away for a moment, when she'd had her first good look at him there in the bright hall. At least it wasn't *just* that.

Tall and broad of shoulder, Vincent Everett had one of those athletic-type bodies that could, if the man didn't have a meticulous tailor, make him look stuffed into the current fashions. The baron's tailor was obviously of the meticulous sort, though, since he cut a fine, dashing figure instead, despite his excess in muscular limbs.

So much, the snow and his greatcoat had concealed from her last night. Black hair, not just black, but darkest pitch, angular cheeks, a strong, decisive chin, a narrow nose, features that fit together so perfectly, it was amazing just how handsome he was.

Still, that was only a small part of what had so rattled her. What had been most disturbing was those golden eyes of his that seemed to talk to her. Unfortunately, everything they said was naughty— Good God, how fanciful. He really had disturbed her beyond rational sense—yet his eyes did seem to be expressing things that weren't proper. A mere trick of the light, no doubt. Certainly not intentional. He probably didn't even know the impression his stare gave others. And it was probably her own heightened emotions that caused her to imagine more than what was really there.

What had been merely a simple business deal for him, just another boring financial transaction, had been a calamity for her in the loss of her home. She couldn't help the antipathy she felt toward him for that. But that strong emotion was probably why everything else he made her feel was much more exaggerated.

As she'd eaten, she had had trouble swallowing each bite. There had been so much churning going on in the region of her belly that she had feared she was going to heave right back up what little food she got down. And yet he had continued to stare. Most rude. Most nerve-racking. Yet because he had done so nearly the entire time she was with him, she had to conclude it wasn't deliberate, wasn't meant to discompose her, was probably just a normal, if rude, habit. Perhaps even a business tactic he had perfected and now unconsciously used in every aspect of his life.

She had seen one merchant try such a tactic on her father once, staring pointedly at him in an effort to cause enough doubt that the price they were negotiating might be raised before verbal commitment was made. It hadn't worked on her father, but it had been amusing to watch.

It took several knocks before the sound broke through Larissa's troubled thoughts and she rose to open the door. Vincent Everett stood there. She had just been hoping that she might be able to avoid any more encounters with him while she was here, yet there he was. And standing so close that she could smell the musky scent of him, feel the heat that he radiated—or was that the heat of her own embarrassment?

She thought to step back, would have run to the far side of the room if it wouldn't point out clearly to him how much he disturbed her. The little space she did gain made no difference, though, because he was doing it again, staring. And such heat in those amber eyes! She had the impression of being completely stripped for his perusal. And the embarrassment was the same as if she really were standing there naked before him.

"Your jewels."

She wondered briefly if he'd just said it, or was repeating himself. She wouldn't be the least surprised.

"Excuse me?"

"I was afraid you might forget." And the look he gave her now said he'd been right, she was a complete scatterbrain. "But I don't want to be indirectly responsible for causing you any more distress, which would be the case if your jewels turn up missing."

That jogged her memory. "Oh, yes, the new servants that haven't proven themselves yet. Just a moment."

She moved quickly to her three large trunks, which had been stacked neatly like a pyramid at the foot of the bed. Rummaging through the one on top didn't reveal her jewel box, but unfortunately, it was the heaviest trunk, since it contained her personal books. This would have been no problem if she had time to unpack it first. But with the baron waiting at the door, it was necessary to move it out of the way to get into the two trunks below it.

She knew very well she couldn't lift the thing herself, but she could drag it off the top with a little effort, and started to do so. But the baron's arms were suddenly on both sides of her, reaching for the handles on the ends of the trunk to move it for her.

He should have said he would do it. He should have let her move out of the way first. Her heart slammed in her chest. She was trapped between him and the trunks, could feel his chest against her back, his breath on her neck. She was going to faint, she knew it, knew it, was going to expire right there on the spot.

"Sorry," he said after an unbearably long moment, and he moved one arm to let her out of his trap.

Again her instinct was to bolt to the other side of the room, far, far away from him. She desperately wanted to, but she refused to let him think she was afraid of him, which was what he would surely think. He was the enemy, after all. And she wasn't afraid, not really. What she felt was far more disturbing than fear.

He set the heavy upper trunk aside, probably could have done so with one hand, it seemed so effortless to him. And he didn't move back to the doorway as would have been proper. They were alone, after all, completely alone, *in a bloody bedroom no less*, which went beyond improper, was in the realm of compromising. So she dove into the next trunk as soon as it was cleared, the sooner to get him out of there, and thankfully came up with the narrow, wooden jewel box this time.

"There are only these few pieces that were my mother's, and her mother's before her," she said as she thrust the box at him. "They are valuable, but the value is more sentimental to me than anything—"

She gasped instead of finishing. He had placed his hand over hers on the box to take it from her, probably because he hadn't taken his eyes off of her long enough to glance down at what he was reaching for. It was a shock to her, staring into his eyes as his warm palm slid over the top of hers, slowly, too slowly, before he finally took the box from her. She was totally undone again, blood racing so fast she really did think she would faint this time.

That touch they had just shared, which had completely shattered her composure, meant absolutely nothing to him. He glanced down as he flipped open the box to look inside at the long strand of pearls and the pearl and ruby butterfly pin therein.

"I understand," he said tonelessly before looking up at her again with gold eyes that seemed even hotter, though it was probably just the light again that made them seem so. "And these?"

Before she realized what he was referring to, or going to do, he flicked one of the earrings she was wearing with his finger. His other fingers brushed against her neck as he did so, an accident surely, yet she felt the shiver clear down to her toes. She swayed as her knees started to buckle. She forgot how to breathe. In a desperate effort to regain control of her senses, she closed her eyes—and heard a groan. His? Surely not.

She focused on the subject, or what she thought was the subject. It took several long moments to dredge it up. The slamming of the lid on the jewel box helped, startled her enough to open her eyes again too.

"The earrings are always with me, either worn or resting beside my bed when I sleep."

"I'm not taking any chances where you are concerned. Give them to me."

It was a harsh order or seemed to be, since his voice had gone quite raspy. Did he mean the earrings? She wasn't sure. She couldn't think clearly again. But just in case, she yanked them off and thrust them at him, then nervously let them drop before his hand actually got close enough, too afraid that she might end up touching him again. It was too soon, though, and he wasn't quite quick enough to catch them before they fell to the floor.

Embarrassed that her nervousness was so very obvious, she thoughtlessly dropped to one knee to pick the earrings up, overlooking the fact that he might do the same. They butted heads on the way down. She lost her balance, ended up sitting on the floor. And before she could recover on her own, he was helping her up.

This was truly her undoing. She was rendered speechless by the shock of it. Instead of offering his hand, which she most certainly wouldn't have taken—he must have known that—he lifted her up, grasping her beneath her armpits, as one would a very small child. It should have been impossible, at least from the floor. But he used his own chest for leverage. And in those brief seconds she felt his palms near the sides of her breasts, felt those breasts pressed firmly to his chest before he let her go. Mere seconds. Yet the impressions would last her an eternity.

The pearls hadn't been picked up yet. He did that now, as well as retrieving the jewel box he'd set down while assisting her. The earrings he closed tightly in his fist rather than put them in the box. For once, he seemed as agitated as she, but it was only a brief display, gone so swiftly, she figured she must have imagined it. He did turn toward the door, however, his errand complete, eager to be gone.

She wouldn't have stopped him. It was crucial that he leave before she fell completely apart. But her mind simply wasn't in its proper working order, and with the trunks still in her view, she recalled . . .

"Oh! I was going to find your housekeeper . . . I seem to have been put in the wrong room. I should be closer to my brother—"

She would have said more, but he interrupted her. "You were situated correctly. I usually have guests over the holidays, and these particular guests can't be made to think they are being given special treatment, you understand, when they are business associates. And rather than move you—if you are still here at that time—it was much easier to just place you here now. Is there a problem with the room?"

"Well, no, but—"

"Good, then think nothing of it."

He continued out the door before she could argue further. The second the door closed, she collapsed on the bed. She was visibly trembling. Her nerves were so frayed she felt like screaming. Her heart was still beating erratically. Good God, what had that man just done to her?

Chapter 6

$\mathcal{V}$incent closed himself in his study, where he could be assured of no interruptions. His staff was well trained, knew not to bother him with incidentals when his door was closed, his secretary being the sole exception. His bedroom would have guaranteed no interruptions at all, but his bedroom was too close to her.

Never in his life had he gotten drunk in the afternoon. Today just might prove an exception. Not that the brandy he had poured for himself seemed to be helping. He had hoped that it would calm him, or at least get his mind off of Larissa Ascot long enough for his body to settle down. It was doing neither.

Just as he shouldn't have gone to her door last night, he most certainly shouldn't have sought her out in her room today. And the jewelry had merely been an excuse for him to do so. He had simply wanted to be in her presence again, had been so stimulated by her during lunch that he was loath to stay away from her when she was nearby.

But that had been a mistake. Seeing her with a bed near to hand had brought The Seduction to mind. It was a perfect setting, after all, to begin it. And he'd thought he could handle it, was even progressing nicely—until he got caught in it himself.

He had never felt desire like this, so completely out of his control. It still amazed him, the strength of it, and the overwhelming urge he'd had to toss her on that nearby bed and ravish her in absolute, unrestrained abandon. Not that he knew much about ravishing, or doing things without restraint, for that matter. But he knew it was too soon to do anything of the sort with her.

She'd been aroused, yes—good God, how easy that had been—and likely would have offered only a token protest before giving in to that arousal. But that was not what he wanted. He wanted her complete surrender, wanted her begging for everything he planned to give her. Her ruination was going to be her own doing, merely helped along by him. His blasted conscience, which seemed to be rearing its silly head at this late stage in his life, wasn't going to be pricked when he was done with her.

He had now removed any other options for her as well, leaving her no choice but to accept his hospitality. He had already arranged for her furniture to be "stolen," which was the story he would give her if she mentioned again needing to sell it. Having had anything of value moved to a separate location, he could even take her to the warehouse where it was stored if necessary, to show her that what remained hadn't been worth stealing, so wasn't worth selling either.

And her jewels would be inaccessible for her, the key to his safe unfortunately "misplaced"—for the time being. He hadn't locked them away yet, though, held one of the earrings in his hand now, unconsciously rubbing it along the side of his cheek. He had watched them sway in her nervousness and thump gently against her neck. They'd still been warm when he'd picked them up, her heat in them, and he'd grasped that warmth tightly in his fist on the way out the door, unwilling to let it go, when he had just forced himself to let *her* go.

It was such a simple plan, this seduction. How in the bloody hell did it suddenly seem so complicated? But he knew why. He hadn't counted on the effect she had on him, hadn't planned on being charmed by her blushes, entranced by her beauty, fascinated by her myriad emotions, nor aroused by an innocent touch and set on fire by her own desire. *He* was the one who had been seduced, and most thoroughly. And he wasn't sure if he could manage to subject himself to that again, without bringing it to a natural conclusion.

He should distance himself, timewise, at least until he could get these unexpected reactions of his under control. Avoid her completely for a day or two. But there was no time for that. No more touching, then. The touching had been his own undoing. Surely he could conduct this seduction without physical contact. Work on her sympathies instead. Even resort to a bit of natural courtship of the less obvious sort. Seduce her mind first, then her body.

Satisfied with the new plan, Vincent finished off

the brandy and didn't refill his glass. And he was glad of the distraction when the knock sounded at the door now. Since it was only his secretary who ever intruded here, it wasn't surprising to see Horace Dudley enter.

Vincent had forgotten, however, that he might need to be looking for a new secretary. A distinctly annoying thought. But just as stiff of form as he'd been last night when he marched off down that snowy street, Horace carried the promised letter of resignation in hand. Vincent didn't give the little man a chance to present it.

"Put that away, Mr. Dudley. I have already rectified what you found so objectionable, leaving you no reason to desert your position here."

"Rectified? You've allowed the Ascots to keep their house?"

Vincent frowned over that absurd conclusion. "After all the effort and favors I called in to acquire it? No. But the lady is staying here until her father returns, so she won't be sitting on some street corner, huddled in a blanket, half-buried in snow."

Horace cleared his throat. "I hadn't quite imagined such a dire circumstance, m'lord, but apparently you did."

Vincent's frown took on deeper lines. "Not a'-tall, and beside the point," he said briskly. "You will agree, however, that you no longer have reason to look for a new position?"

After the tongue-lashing he had received from his wife last night over his high morals, which wouldn't put bread on the table, Horace was happy to say, "Indeed, and thank you, m'lord."

"Back to work, then. You may concentrate now on those two investments we discussed last week. Oh, and summon my physician to the house."

"You are feeling poorly?"

"No, but let the staff know that he'll be here to take care of any illness or physical complaints they might have."

"You should know they won't come forward, m'lord. Physicians are much too expensive for minor—"

"I'll take care of the charges."

Horace blinked. "That's quite—generous of you. Are you sure you aren't feeling poorly?"

The frown became a definite scowl. "I haven't gone daft, man, and I always have ulterior motives. Just make sure, if he's asked by Miss Ascot, that he tells her he sees to the staff here each year at this time. And have him look in on her brother while he's here. The boy has apparently been sick for some time now."

"Ah, now I understand. You don't want her to feel indebted to you."

Vincent almost laughed at the misconception. Indebted would be nice, but would have to wait for something else to inspire it. His only concern now was to keep the lady from trying to pay for a physician herself. Horace didn't need to know that, however, so Vincent merely nodded, allowing him to think what he would.

Chapter 7

$\mathcal{V}$incent managed to distract himself for the remainder of the afternoon. But by the time the dinner hour was approaching, he was so filled with anticipation of seeing his beautiful houseguest again that he knew damn well he didn't dare. Not yet. Not when just the thought of her entering the room set his blood to racing.

Bloody hell. This just wouldn't do. There was the chance she might not come down to share the meal with him. But just in case she felt common courtesy would demand it, he left the house. There was only one cure for his current dilemma, and there were several residences where he could find it.

He decided upon Lady Catherine. A widow of several years, she never failed to welcome him into her home. And since she was somewhat of a recluse, he rarely found her already entertaining when he called on her, as tended to be the case with the other women he shared company with. He didn't keep a mistress, had never found the need to when he had so many invitations from the women of his acquaintance that he couldn't keep track of them all. The few he regularly visited were the least complicated of the lot, enjoyed the independence that widowhood gave them, and wanted from him no more than he was willing to give, or at least strived to give that impression.

Catherine was a handsome woman a few years older than Vincent. She was indebted to him. He had arranged for her to acquire the house of her dreams, the one she had fallen in love with as a child and had wanted ever since. She had been unable to convince the owner to sell to her when she'd become a rich widow. It was how Vincent had met her, when he'd heard what she was after.

He hadn't lied to Larissa when he'd told her

how he made his fortune. Catherine had paid him an exorbitant fee for finding out what it would take to get the owner of the house to sell—in that particular case, a racing stable in Kent which the man had never thought to acquire himself, even though he was an avid horseman, and an invitation to meet the queen, both easily obtainable.

Catherine was still indebted, or felt she was. She really did love her house. Vincent often wondered if that was why there was always plenty of extra food available when he showed up unexpectedly, even though Catherine would otherwise have eaten alone.

The lavish meal, he enjoyed as usual, for she had a splendid cook. He even enjoyed her company, her fine wit able to amuse him occasionally, when he was a man who didn't find much amusing. She expected him to stay the night with her. He had planned to. It was why he was there. But as much as he had been overcome with desire that day, he felt absolutely none that evening.

It wasn't Catherine's fault. She was as lovely and accommodating as usual. It was Larissa's fault. She still wouldn't leave his thoughts, even for the few hours he spent with another woman.

He left directly after the meal. Catherine was disappointed and had trouble hiding it, though she tried. He'd never done that before. But had he stayed, he probably would have embarrassed them both.

He returned home with dread, though, knowing full well that he was going to have a problem with Larissa's close proximity that night. How utterly insane, to have put her in that particular room, with no locks on the doors between them. There were no guests expected over the holidays. He had wanted her where he could reach her. He had been thinking, foolishly, of *after* The Seduction, when he expected to continue to share her bed, at least until her father's return, and so had arranged the easiest access to it. He had *not* counted on being tempted beyond reason before he had her.

He'd been right. He was unable to sleep. He'd been right, too, that he'd be unable to resist entering her room that night. He had an excuse ready, in case she awoke. She didn't. She slept very soundly. He didn't even try to be quiet, wanted her to wake. She didn't. She was driving him crazy.

Somehow, and he'd never know where he dredged up the will, he managed to get out of there without disturbing her. He even managed to get to sleep, probably because it was now near dawn. He'd actually spent most of the night in her room in a state of heightened anticipation that had finally drained him to exhaustion.

And he dreamed that she stood at the foot of his bed, watching him sleep, as he had done to her . . .

It wasn't a dream. Larissa had been unable to sleep as well, though in her case, she didn't know what was bothering her so much that all she could do was toss and turn and pound on her pillow every few minutes in vexation that sleep was avoiding her. She'd heard Vincent come down the hall, had known it was he, because their doors were the only ones at the end of the hall. She'd heard vague sounds after that, nothing distinguishable— until the inner door to her room opened and she went so still, she briefly forgot to breathe.

It was he, and all those feelings he had ac-quainted her with that afternoon came back, just knowing he was there. She couldn't imagine what he wanted, wasn't going to ask. When she realized he wasn't going to wake her to tell her, no amount of curiosity got her to open her eyes. She pretended sleep. She didn't want to know, really didn't.

Her heart pounded so loudly she was sure he

must hear it, and still he didn't wake her. He made enough noise that she probably would have woken easily—if she weren't pretending to sleep. Then he was quiet, so quiet, she could no longer be sure he was still there. Yet she couldn't relax, wouldn't open her eyes to find out for certain, either. A wise choice, because when he did finally leave several hours later, she heard him clearly, heard his sigh, too.

She unwound with the closing of the door. She hadn't known she'd been so tense the whole while, and was sure to be stiff for it in the morning. But instead of turning over and finally getting to sleep herself, she found herself following behind the baron. Not immediately. She did *not* want to come face-to-face with him after that nerve-racking ordeal. Yet slowly she passed through the dressing room and into the bathroom, then stood at the door there that connected to his room, with her ear pressed to it.

Ten minutes passed, twenty. Her ear was starting to ache. The room was cold, too far away from the fireplace in the other room to have caught any of its warmth, the portable brazier in the corner unlit. Shivers were already passing down her spine in continuous trips. And then she did what would very likely be the most stupid thing she had ever done or ever would do. She opened his door.

She told herself she just wanted to be assured that he had gone to bed, that he wasn't coming back. Yet when she saw him lying there in his big bed, she was drawn forward despite better sense that warned her not to.

She was mesmerized. There was enough light from the fire he had restoked to see him clearly. His room was warm as well, which was why she didn't leave immediately. At least that was the excuse she gave herself for standing there at the foot of his bed, staring at him. That his chest was bare, even of a blanket, had nothing to do with it.

It was *such* a wide chest. Lightly sprinkled with hair, though because the hair was as pitch black as that on his head, it seemed a much thicker mat. He really did have the body of a man who enjoyed athletic endeavors quite often. His upper arms were as thick as small tree trunks; even his neck was thickly corded.

His jaw was dusted with dark stubble. He must have to shave more than once a day. Her father's facial hair was like that, grew back so quickly that, like most men, he simply sported a beard and merely kept it trim. She wondered why the baron didn't, wondered so many things about him. Was he lonely without family? Whom did he talk to when he needed a friend? Did he have a lady in mind to start a family? Someone he was already courting? Did he even want a family of his own someday? He must. He had a title to pass on. Didn't titled gentlemen take that sort of thing quite seriously?

Not that she would ever ask him any of that. Not that she really cared, was only mildly curious. It was perfectly natural to wonder about the man who had evicted her from her home, then offered temporary lodgings in his own—and caused her so many unusual feelings.

He stirred. She thought his eyes might even have opened, though it was hard to tell. But her heart was suddenly slamming in her chest again. She ducked down behind the bed and crouched there for what seemed an eternity. Even so, she pretty much crawled out of there on all fours, to keep from his immediate view. Her cheeks were flaming. Common sense had returned. She knew she had done a stupid, stupid thing and wasn't taking any more chances.

Chapter 8

$\mathcal{I}$t was a muffled thud, coming from beyond two closed doors, but it was enough to wake Larissa. She didn't find out what the noise had been, though, until she wandered, blurry eyed, into the bathroom, and found one of the household footmen kneeling on the floor there in front of the door that connected to the baron's room.

The man's presence startled her to full wakefulness. Wide-eyed now, she just managed to cut off a shriek of surprise, in fact.

But a thorough glance revealed his tools and that he had been installing locks on the doors. It was the doorknob on the one he was working on, accidentally falling to the marble floor, that had made the noise that woke her.

This he apologized for profusely while he explained in embarrassment that he was supposed to have been finished with his task before she arose, so he wouldn't disturb her. Walking in and finding a man in her bathroom was indeed disturbing, though not nearly so much as it would have been if the man had been the baron instead.

The housekeeper was there as well, supervising, though on the other side of the door in the baron's room. She made her own presence known by dragging the footman out of there for the time being.

Her parting remark cleared up any remaining confusion, or it should have. "He'll finish up, miss, when you go down for lunch. The baron wasn't aware that these doors were without locks. Didn't think of it myself, either. Nothing wrong with that, of course, if a wife were installed, but with a guest, well, you understand . . ."

Larissa understood perfectly, the *need* for a lock on each of the two bathroom doors. What she didn't understand was why they were being installed now, after the fact, as it were. And at the baron's request, obviously.

The lack of locks was most likely why she had been unable to get to sleep last night to begin with. She realized that now. She'd tried to lock the doors as soon as she had retired to her room last night. That she couldn't must have added to her unease at being in a strange house—with very good reason as it turned out.

But with the baron installing locks, she had to wonder what really happened last night. She had assumed it was he who had entered her room, but she hadn't opened her eyes, not once, to make sure. And then it occurred to her, who else it could have been.

One of those new servants that hadn't proven themselves yet. The baron had been worried enough about them to have her lock up her jewelry. One of them could well have been trying to rob her last night, but didn't leave in time when she showed up for bed. The thieving maid could have hid in the dressing room until she was asleep, then tried to sneak out.

Fear could have frozen the thief in her room— or she realized Larissa wasn't asleep. She hadn't moved, after all, not once, in her pretense. The maid could have been waiting in an agony of fear for Larissa to make some kind of sleep sound to assure her she wasn't awake, yet she never did. And opening the outer door to the hall would have brought in some light. Had she been awake, she most certainly would have started screaming, or so the thief could have thought.

It was a perfectly viable explanation, much more realistic, really, than that the baron had stood there for hours by her bed, watching her sleep as she had thought. And the thief had finally given up with that sigh she had heard and gone back into the dressing room to hide the rest of the night, because Larissa never did stir enough to let her think she could escape without her notice.

Yet she had given the thief her escape when she had, soon after that, entered the bathroom to listen at the baron's door. The maid could have slipped out of her room with ease then. Larissa wouldn't have heard her. She was listening for sounds on the other side of the door, not behind her.

Good God, the baron must have seen her in his room last night, and *that* was why locks were going on the doors this morning. And he'd been there all along in his room. She was the one who had intruded, without reason, or without reason from his perspective.

Larissa groaned and buried her face in her hands. She was never leaving that room. No, she couldn't stay there, it wasn't really her room. But she was never going to face the baron again. Couldn't. Such embarrassment went beyond anything of her experience.

She'd leave his house. She had to. He was kind enough not to insist on it himself, had ordered locks instead. But she simply couldn't stay there now and risk seeing him again. What he must be thinking—how utterly mortifying.

And then she groaned again. To leave, she *had* to see him. He had her jewels in his safe. He also had the address where the rest of their possessions had been taken. She couldn't get either without speaking to him. And if she had to speak to him, she was going to have to explain to him what had happened last night.

Had she ever dreaded anything so much? She didn't think so. But prevaricating had put her in this mess to begin with. If she had sold the jewels sooner, or started selling off the furnishings, she would have had a bit of money on hand to take them to a hotel until she could figure out what to do, instead of coming here.

Having inquired of the first servant she passed the baron's whereabouts, she was taken to his study downstairs. She was told he could be found there most mornings after he returned from his daily ride, though not often in the afternoons, when he made social and business calls elsewhere. Today was an exception.

She wasn't really listening to the servant's chatter as she was led there. Her cheeks were already flaming in anticipation of seeing Lord Everett. She had to force one foot in front of the other to walk into his presence.

It was a nice-looking office, accommodating, the chairs about the room designed for comfort rather than just utility, so anyone who joined him there would feel at ease—at least anyone but her. Several lamps had been lit, since the day had turned out quite dark and dreary, with snow still falling in short bursts. The rose-colored lamp domes went quite well with the ruby drapes. She was trying to look at anything but him, but that didn't last long.

He sat behind a large desk. He was reading a newspaper. He didn't glance up. It was probably no more than a reflection from the lamp on the desk beside him, with its rose shade, that made his cheeks look as pink as hers must be. Wishful thinking, to hope he was embarrassed, too.

"Someone was in my room last night. I thought it was you, but you were sleeping."

She blurted it out—and realized, too late, that she was *admitting* to having entered his room in the middle of the night. How else could she have known he was sleeping? Had he not known of her intrusion, he certainly did now.

"It could have been me."

It took several long moments before that statement broke through her embarrassment, and then she blinked in confusion. "Excuse me? 'Could have' implies you don't know. How is that possible?"

"I've never awakened to find myself walking about, yet I've been assured that I do just that on occasion, take strolls while I'm asleep. Not often. And I don't go far, apparently. If I did, I would have to consider having myself locked in at night, which I would rather not do. But it did occur to me that

I might wander into your room during one of these strange occurrences, which is why I ordered the locks, to prevent any chance of that happening."

He was taking the blame on himself, even if he wasn't at fault. She was relieved by his explanation. Her embarrassment even subsided. He hadn't seen her. And she had the means to secure the room on all sides now, whether she was in it or not, so she wouldn't have to worry about thieves either. He had removed her reason to leave.

She should still leave. There was something just not right about her feelings for the baron. She should despise him and nothing more, yet there was more.

She almost said as much, that she would begin immediately looking for other accommodations. But then she remembered her brother, and the new physician who had examined him yesterday, assuring her that he should be up and about in no more than a week—if he continued his present convalescence. And he had stressed, repeatedly, just as their own doctor had, that Thomas was to avoid drafts at all costs, which might cause him a relapse.

She had forgotten all that in the misery of her

embarrassment, which was still another reason why they should leave the baron's house. He simply filled her mind too much, to the exclusion of all else.

She could wait at least another week, though, for her brother's full recovery. But in the meantime, she could find an auction house that would assist her in disposing of the more valuable furnishings, and a jeweler who would offer her a fair price for her mother's pearls. She could no longer depend on her father coming home to make everything right again for them, when she had finally admitted to herself that he might never be coming home.

She was also going to have to obtain employment to support herself and Thomas. Their father's numerous assets were going to be denied them until he was officially declared . . . She couldn't say it, even in thought. But she had no idea how long that would take.

A quick glance out the window reminded her that it was rather late to get started on all of that today, nor was it a pleasant day to be walking about London, when the snow that had begun to fall last night continued to appear periodically. The last thing she needed was to catch a cold and end up confined to a bed herself. In the morning, then—if she could manage a normal night's sleep.

She made haste now to leave the baron's presence. "I'm sorry to have bothered you. I'll leave you to your reading now. And thank you for thinking of the locks."

"Don't go."

Chapter 9

It was jolting, hearing that "Don't go" from Lord Everett, particularly since Larissa had just been thinking about leaving his house. It took a moment to realize he meant for her not to leave his study, rather than his house. It still had sounded plaintive, his tone, almost desperate, which was why it had been so jarring to her.

He *was* lonely. She was sure of that now. It shouldn't bother her, though. He was nothing to her, after all; no, worse, he was a despicable, evicting landlord. Unfortunately, her heart, soft as it was, ignored that. It did bother her that he was lonely; it went right to the core of her compassionate nature.

She glanced back at him, raised a questioning brow to force him to elaborate. That seemed to confound him. He needed a reason to keep her there, but apparently didn't have one handy. His request had been impulsive, and had revealed too much of himself. She took pity and moved toward the window, giving him more time to find his "reason."

She expected to hear something trite, but in the end he surprised her, even made her rethink her conclusion that he was lonely, for which she was quite glad. She didn't *want* to feel any sympathy for him, after all.

It was a subject that he no doubt intended to cover with her, and it could merely have slipped his mind for a moment, which had given her the wrong impression. But he knew he had something to bring up, had asked her to stay so he could, then couldn't recall what it was.

Perfectly logical; it happened to everyone on occasion. For her to have surmised that he was lonely, merely because a subject eluded him for a moment, was rather far-fetched on her part.

Wishful thinking again? Absurd. She merely needed to stop making assumptions about him.

"Did my physician attend to your brother yesterday?" was his forgotten question.

"Yes."

"Good. I wanted to make sure that my servants didn't keep him so busy that he might have run out of time to see everyone who needed his attention, but he left before I could speak to him."

She smiled. "No, I believe he mentioned that Thomas was his first patient of the day."

"And the boy's progress?"

"Still recovering nicely, though he must continue bed rest for another week or so."

"He must have deplored that news."

"Ah, you remember what it was like to be that age?" she replied.

It was a natural question following his remark, yet it brought an immediate frown to his brow that she couldn't help wondering about. She refused to ask what caused it, though. The less she knew about him, the better off she would be, she was sure.

So she continued as if he hadn't just caused her a great deal of curiosity. "Yes, Tommy hates having to remain in bed. He's never been this ill before, at least not with anything that required such a lengthy convalescence, which is why I try to spend as much time with him as I can. We also had to let go his tutor, so I've been filling in there as well. Though with nothing better to do, Tommy is so far ahead in his studies, I don't know why I bother."

"Intelligent boy?"

The frown had left as quickly as it came, making her think she might have imagined it. "Very. It was why he was being taught at home. The headmaster of his last school refused to advance him to a higher age group, yet what he was being taught was nothing that he didn't already know."

"Such decisions can be made for other than academic reasons," he pointed out.

"We're aware that Tommy will have a difficult time with his peers, if he enters college too young. The teasing began long ago from those his age, because his thinking is more adult in nature than childlike. He will probably work with our father for a few years, then enter college at the appropriate age—at least that was . . ."

She couldn't finish, having touched on the probability again that her father wouldn't be there in the future. Nor had she even thought yet what his continued absence was going to do to his business.

The shipping company wouldn't be turned over to her for disposal until he was officially declared dead, yet in the meantime it would fail, so there would be nothing left to turn over. She couldn't run it herself, didn't have the necessary knowledge to do so. Thomas was too young yet to take over. And the clerk who had been left in charge couldn't continue indefinitely either, making decisions that were beyond his capabilities.

"That was the plan?" the baron guessed, unwilling to leave the subject alone. "Before what?"

"Before these rumors started, that my father isn't going to return."

There was a moment of silence as her eyes glistened with unshed tears which he couldn't help but notice. "You think he's dead, don't you?"

"No!"

Too much emphasis. Too much despair. An obvious lie which he ignored.

"There are countless reasons that could have detained him, none of which include any dire circumstances," he told her. "You have been inconvenienced by the delay, but there is no reason to think it is anything other than a delay."

The word he'd chosen, "inconvenienced," almost brought forward a bitter laugh from her. Was that how he viewed an eviction, as no more than an inconvenience to the tenant? Yet she did realize that he was trying to bolster her hope, which she had finally abandoned. She just wished she could borrow some of his optimism, but it didn't work. Her own had sustained her this long, but was now gone.

She couldn't talk to him anymore. The lump in her throat was all but choking her. But there was nothing more to say. She'd already answered his reason for detaining her, that and more.

And then she looked at him. A mistake. She should have walked out while she still had some of her wits about her. She might have been able to manage a few words in parting at the door. But looking at him, she saw the concern in his golden eyes that he probably didn't realize was there, and burst into tears. Impossible to stop. Impossible to control.

It was too far from the window to the door. She didn't make it before his hand was on her shoulder, stopping her, then his arms were gathering her close.

It was what she had needed for several weeks now, a shoulder to cry on. That it was the shoulder of the very person responsible for some of those tears pouring out of her didn't seem to matter much.

He held her close, and tightly, as if he were over-come with emotion himself. He wasn't, surely. He was just trying to comfort her and probably wasn't sure how to go about it, was probably quite unac-customed to women falling apart in front of him.

It *was* comforting, having his arms around her, his solid chest to lean on, and so nice that she was loath to end it. But when the tears started to dry up, she started to become aware of him in a differ-ent way, in the way that so disturbed her and rat-tled her common sense.

She stepped back quickly, breaking his warm embrace. "Thank you, I'm fine now."

She wasn't, but it was the correct thing to say to him. Unfortunately, he was too perceptive, and blunt enough to remark on it.

"You aren't."

She really was, at least for the moment, in the

matter that had needed comfort. It was something else altogether making her tremble now. And she was afraid to look at him directly, to see what was in his eyes this time. She suspected that it would be a terrible risk, to subject herself to that molten fire if it was there again. Her emotions were just too fragile at the moment to withstand it.

So she turned away toward the open doorway and even passed through it before she said, "I *will* be."

Whether he heard her, or would have argued the point, was moot. She didn't give him a chance to, practically ran all the way to her room.

Chapter 10

*L*arissa had been told last evening, when she had gone down to dinner and had eaten it alone, that the baron usually wasn't at home in the evenings. Quite understandable for a member of the *ton*, particularly during one of the more prominent social Seasons, which was in full swing, to be attending one social gathering or another. So he rarely ate at home, which for her had been good news.

It was why she went downstairs tonight. She wasn't expecting to see him again that day. Besides, she had no reason to offer to take her meals in her room, so it would be quite rude to do so.

He joined her.

Having assumed he wouldn't, it was quite disconcerting, watching him walk into the room, offer her a curt nod, and take his seat across from her. Her embarrassment returned over the outburst of tears he'd been witness to that afternoon. Horrid emotion, to be so uncontainable and embarrass her like that. But at the time she hadn't thought of that, hadn't thought of anything except the grief pouring out of her.

He wasn't going to remark on it, though, for which she was most grateful. He said a few words to the servant who poured his wine. She had declined wine herself, didn't usually drink it with dinner, but she caught the servant's eye now and indicated she'd changed her mind. She needed something, anything, to help her get through this meal, now that she wouldn't be having it alone.

The silence between them was embarrassing in itself. They ought to be talking to each other. It was the civilized thing to do. Surely she could manage some normal conversation that wouldn't lead to a burst of emotion. And she had Thomas's request still in mind.

He'd asked her again today about adding their Christmas decorations to the baron's tree. She didn't plan to be here for Christmas, hoped to find other accommodations by then, though she didn't tell Thomas that. And just in case she had trouble finding a suitable place in time, she really ought to cover the subject with the baron.

It was a simple request, after all. Nor could she imagine why he might deny it. And it was conversation! Desperately needed, because the continued silence was beginning to heat her cheeks.

She began, "I've noticed you haven't brought in a tree yet for Christmas. When do you usually decorate one?"

"I don't," he replied simply as he sat back with his wineglass in hand and gave her his full attention.

She should have realized that. She simply couldn't imagine him doing anything so festive. He no doubt left the task to his servants, then merely enjoyed their efforts.

So she rephrased her question. "But when do you usually have one decorated?"

"I don't," he replied yet again.

She was so surprised she couldn't hide it. "Are you saying you don't have a tree put up—ever?"

He raised a brow at her. "Why are you having trouble with that fact?"

"Because—I've never not had a Christmas tree myself. I thought everyone . . . But how did you celebrate Christmas as a child?"

"I didn't."

She thought of her own many Christmas experiences as a child, the fun in decorating a tree, the excitement as presents gathered under it . . . That he had never experienced any of that, she simply couldn't comprehend.

"You *are* English, aren't you?"

He laughed. She saw nothing funny in the subject. Thomas was looking forward to decorating a tree with his own lovingly crafted ornaments. He *would* have a tree to do so if she had to go out and cut one down herself.

"Quite English," he answered after his laughter wound down to a smile. "I merely never had anyone to share the holiday with."

She blushed. "I'm sorry, I didn't know you were orphaned that young."

118

"I wasn't," he said with a shrug. "My parents died after I had reached twenty."

Larissa stared at him. She also gave up. His family must have simply been—strange.

If he had a wife, the lady would insist on a tree. With that thought occurring, she asked him, "Why have you not married yet?"

It was the wine. She never would have asked such a personal question if she hadn't gulped down her first glass of wine and was already working on the second, nor asked it so bluntly. She wished the footman with the wine bottle would go away. No, actually, she wished he were standing closer rather than so far across the room, he wasn't even within hearing distance.

The baron didn't take offense, though; he even answered her. "I have yet to find a compelling reason to marry."

She should have apologized for the personal question, instead pointed out, "But you have a title to pass on."

"My father's title. I despised him, so why would I want to preserve his title?"

"That's rather harsh," she replied. "Surely you didn't really."

"You're quite right. The hate didn't last more than a few years. Indifference prevailed thereafter."

"You're serious, aren't you? I've never known anyone to not love their parents."

It was probably her surprise that made him chuckle. "You've led a sheltered life, Larissa. You've never known anyone to not have a Christmas tree either. Shall I tell you how easy it is for both to occur?"

She should have said no. Knowing more about him was not going to be good for her peace of mind, she was sure . . .

"Yes."

He finished off his own wine before he began. "I grew up on the family estate in Lincolnshire, which I haven't been back to since my parents died."

"Why?"

"Because I have nothing but feelings of inadequacy there, and the memories that caused them."

She changed her mind abruptly. "You don't have to delve into those memories—"

"It's quite all right," he interrupted. "Believe me, those feelings are gone. In fact, I have no feelings remaining at all, where my parents are concerned. They were social butterflies. They did

120

their duty in producing the required heir, myself, then proceeded to ignore me. I was turned over to servants to raise. Quite a normal occurrence, in the *ton*."

That was true, she supposed, though not as frequent as his "normal" implied. Nor did it explain why he had hated his parents, but she didn't need to point that out, because he continued.

"My brother, Albert, came along a few years after me, unplanned, unwanted really, and turned over to the servants as well. Consistent of them, so I didn't realize yet that my parents simply didn't like children, at least had no time to share with them. They were never at home, after all, so neither of us was actually ignored, it was more like we were—forgotten. I even became close to Albert briefly, before they took him away."

"Away?"

"With them. You see, by his fourth year, he became the 'court jester.' It's how I've always thought of him. He went out of his way to amuse people—and succeeded. He was quite good at it. While I, on the other hand, had no such qualities. I was too serious, too reserved. If I ever laughed as a child, I don't remember it.

"On one of my parents' rare visits, they discovered this. They had brought home guests. Albert managed to make most of these guests laugh. He was entertaining. My parents suddenly found him of value in their socializing, and worth spending time with, so of course, he must travel with them."

"But not you," she said in a quiet tone, not a question, an obvious summation.

"No, certainly, I was the heir and already being tutored. And I wasn't amusing. But they did finally bring Albert home, when he had to begin his own schooling. And they came to visit much more often, stayed for months at a time now. They missed Albert, after all. And when he wasn't in school, they took him off again with them."

"On holidays," she guessed, holidays like Christmas.

"Yes."

Larissa felt like crying—for him. He had said it all matter-of-factly. It meant nothing to him now. But dear Lord, it must have bothered him as a child, when his brother was lavished with attention, and he was given none. Inadequate, he had mentioned. Yes, he would have felt that, would have felt left out, unloved, unwanted . . .

She cried anyway, couldn't stop it despite trying to, silent tears, at least, that she was able to quickly swipe away before he noticed—or he was pretending not to notice. He probably hadn't liked having to offer comfort to her that afternoon, and didn't want to have to do so again. He wouldn't attribute her tears to anything to do with him, thankfully. Why would he, when they barely knew each other? He'd think she was thinking of her father again—if he even noticed the new tears.

Stupid, stupid emotions, to have her crying like a ninny so frequently these days. But she felt so sorry for Lord Everett, to have had such a horrid childhood, such a cold and unloving family.

He must hate his brother, too, if he was still living. He'd said their closeness had only been brief. And that left him no one. He was so alone—so in need of someone to care about him.

"So you see now why I have never celebrated Christmas," he ended.

She did indeed, and nearly cried again. She really was going to have to work on this emotional weakness of hers, as soon as she figured out how one became hard and indifferent—like the baron was. And her immediate problem hadn't been solved either, so she mentioned it.

"My brother has been raised in a more . . . traditional—manner."

He raised a brow at her. "You're saying you intend to celebrate Christmas—here?"

"Certainly, *if* we are still here."

"And that will require a tree?"

She sighed. "Yes."

"By all means, then. I wouldn't want the boy to not have what he's accustomed to."

"Thank you. We'll put it up in his room, if you'd rather not have it downstairs in the parlor."

"Nonsense, might as well do it right, if you're going to do it."

"We'll need our decorations. They were stored in the attic—"

"I'll have them fetched."

"You're very kind."

He burst out laughing. "No, my dear Larissa, I can be called many things, but kind would certainly never be one of them."

Chapter 11

Vincent found out only after Larissa had left his house that she was gone. Her brother was still there, as were her clothes, so he didn't panic. She obviously meant to come back. He was still annoyed, since he had planned to advance his seduction that morning.

Too much progress had been made yesterday for him not to take advantage of it, and before it became redundant. She had revealed how vulnerable she was in his study, that her father's continued absence had become more than just a worry to her. Such grief made her ripe for comforting, and comforting could come in many forms.

He had offered the most basic form yesterday, no easy task for him, to hold her like that, feel her body trembling, and then let her go. She had felt so right in his arms. He'd never experienced that rightness before.

Her tears and grief were real; he hadn't doubted that for a moment. He just didn't think they were necessary yet, so they hadn't affected him much. She might doubt her father's return, but he didn't, which was why he was still under a time constraint, to get her seduced soonest, before Ascot came to collect her.

If he thought otherwise . . . well, there would no longer be the need for any further revenge on his part. Seducing her was going to ultimately hurt the father. If the father was dead, it would only hurt her—a thought he shied away from. Not that she wouldn't still find a husband eventually. She was too beautiful to remain unmarried for long—another thought he shied away from.

It was really too bad that her father had to be such an underhanded bastard. And amazing that he had raised such a caring, compassionate daughter. Was the son the same, or was it only from the mother's influence, which had been denied the boy? Vincent's reports revealed that she had died with the second child's birth. But Larissa would have had eight years in the mother's care, long enough for her to have developed the softer qualities of her gender.

Compassion had poured out of her last night. He had never thought how deplorable his childhood would seem to someone else. He had lived it, but had put it behind him. Even speaking of it wouldn't bring up those old feelings of pain and loneliness that he had buried so deep in order to survive them. But she had envisioned it all and had cried—for him.

What he had told her was the truth, but just a brief version of it. To no one would he ever admit how many nights he had cried himself to sleep as a child, or the anguish in thinking it was *his* fault that his parents didn't love him, or the misery each time he stood alone at the window and watched them ride away with Albert, leaving him behind. To experience, every time they had had to deal with him, their impatience to have it done so they could continue with more interesting endeavors.

To never have had a single hug or tender touch, even from his mother.

It was nothing to Vincent now because he wouldn't let it be. He had made of his heart a rock void of emotion—in self-defense. But that Larissa would cry for him, when she had so many bitter feelings against him that should take precedent, still amazed him.

He had done his best to ignore those tears, because he didn't want her getting defensive about it, which would have ruined the effect it had had on her. But he did mean to take advantage before she had time to remember why she should spare him no sympathy at all.

So he became annoyed that she wasn't available that morning. Yet when several hours passed and she hadn't returned, he began to worry.

It could not have been a simple walk she was doing. That wouldn't have taken this long. She must have some purpose. Yet she had gone out alone, without escort. London was no place for a young woman, and especially one as beautiful as she was, to walk about alone.

He finally sent people out to look for her. When that produced no results, he went out himself to try to find her. He questioned the neighbors at her old address. He went to the docks to her father's company office, which was nearly deserted now, with only a single clerk remaining. He even went by the warehouse where he had stored her possessions, even though he knew that was pointless, since he hadn't given her the address of it yet, but he'd run out of options.

By the time he returned home, only to be informed she *still* hadn't shown up yet, he acknowledged that his worry was getting out of hand. He went straightaway to her brother's room, which he should have done sooner. If anyone would know where she had gone or why, the boy would.

He found the child abed, propped up with pillows and reading a hefty volume of Greek mythology, of all things, surely not by choice, though no one was with him at the moment to insist. Took his studies seriously, did he? Or perhaps he was simply so intelligent that he craved knowledge constantly, of any sort.

These were vague thoughts that didn't last more than a second due to Vincent's own craving for knowledge—about Larissa. "Where is your sister?"

He should have at least introduced himself first,

realized that with the blank stare he was getting and started to correct the oversight. "I'm—"

"I'm sure I know who you would be, Lord Everett," Thomas interrupted without the least change of expression. "My question is what is it that you require of my sister that has you so impatient to see her?"

"I am not the least bit impatient."

The book was set aside. The boy even crossed his arms in a manner that indicated he would wait until he heard the correct answer. And his direct gaze was actually disconcerting. For a moment Vincent felt as if he were in the presence of the girl's grandfather, rather than her ten-year-old brother. A brief moment.

In a tone gone stiff, Vincent explained, "While you both reside in my house, you are afforded my protection, which makes you more or less my responsibility for the time being. Yet I can't assure her safety if she intends to traipse about London by herself."

"Does she know you are accepting responsibility for her?" Thomas asked.

"I assume—"

The boy interrupted again with the offering, "You can't assume where Rissa is concerned."

"Regardless, she has been missing since early this morning. Is that a normal habit of hers, to go about town without an escort?"

"No indeed, she rarely goes about town at all. She's been quite the recluse, my sister, since we moved to London. Wasn't always the case, least not in Portsmouth. Think this city intimidates her."

"Then why the devil would she go out in it alone?" That question merely gained a shrug from the boy, prompting Vincent to clarify, "You have no idea, then, where she might have gone today?"

"Possibly to collect our Christmas decorations? I'm afraid I have been nagging her—"

Vincent interrupted impatiently this time. "No, I told her I would have them fetched."

"Then to my father's office?"

"No, the clerk there said she hadn't been by," Vincent replied.

"You've already been searching for her?"

This was asked with a raised brow that looked quite odd on a ten-year-old face. Yet the implication was still there that the boy had just drawn conclusions from that information that were no doubt wrong, yet drawn nonetheless.

"Did I mention responsibility?" Vincent almost

growled. "I thought so. Of *course* I would find it necessary to look for her, when she's bloody well been gone for half the day."

"Do you realize how upset you sound, Lord Everett? Do you take all of your responsibilities this seriously? Or just my sister?"

Vincent sighed and got out of there. He wasn't used to dealing with children, and he certainly wasn't used to dealing with little adults in child form. Silly boy, to try and credit Vincent with emotions, of any sort.

Chapter 12

$\mathcal{L}$arissa was walking in the house just as Vincent came downstairs again. She looked cold. She looked tired. She was windblown and damp from snow drizzles that she'd probably been caught in more than once. She was infinitely beautiful even with wind-chapped cheeks.

The anger came immediately to replace the worry he'd undergone, now that he could see she was unharmed, and he blasted her with it the second he reached her. "Don't *ever* leave this house again without taking one of the footmen with you! Do you have no sense at all, to not realize what could happen to you out on those bloody streets?"

She stared at him, and stared. She was probably too tired to muster any expression. Finally she said simply, "They aren't my footmen to command."

"Then consider them henceforth at your beck and call—!" he growled, only to be cut off.

"Nor did I have a choice in the matter. I had to go out . . . so I went."

He gritted his teeth. "There is no 'had to' involved. The only rational choice would have been to stay indoors on a day like this."

"That wouldn't have found me a jeweler willing to pay a fair price for my pearls, nor an auction house interested in the paintings and other objects of art I mean to dispose of," she told him.

Vincent almost panicked. He'd already assured her that she didn't need to sell anything. There had to be a reason that she'd subjected herself to horrid weather and risked her own personal safety. He was either frightening her away, or she was running from things she didn't understand.

She was an innocent. She might not realize yet that the strong feelings she had been experiencing were sexual in nature and perfectly normal. Yet he couldn't explain—and end up frightening her even more.

There was no need to panic, though, since he'd already planned to let her think that her valuables had been stolen or were otherwise unavailable to barter for currency. He would have preferred not to have to lie to her about them, but wouldn't feel too much remorse in doing so. Any means to keep her under his roof was permissible, as far as he was concerned, short of locking her in.

"I thought I assured you that you are most welcome to stay here until your father returns."

"And if he doesn't return?" she asked in a quavering voice. "No, Lord Everett, we can't continue to accept your charity, which is what it is. You required an address of us. That is why we are here. But I assure you I will have an address for you before we leave—I just need to go out and find one, which I intend to do."

"Nonsense," he countered. "You can at least wait until the beginning of the New Year. Surely you can give your father a few more weeks to make an appearance. Or do you mean to disrupt your brother's Christmas as well as his recovery, when you don't have to? And after we just agreed that you shall have your Christmas tree?"

She worried at her lower lip in indecision, seriously chewed on it. He wished she hadn't, because he now had an overwhelming urge to help her chew on it. Such lovely lips she had. Did she realize what her simple action was doing to him?

"I suppose a few weeks more—"

Vincent gave in to the urge. He had meant to further his seduction today, to draw it closer to the inevitable conclusion. And he could see no reason, really, to wait any longer for that conclusion. Once she shared his bed, there would be no more talk of leaving, which was the deciding factor for him. And the sooner she did, the longer he would have to enjoy her, before her father arrived to take her away.

He didn't expect to lose himself so deeply in the magic of his own creation, but he did. He wouldn't have carried her straight upstairs either, where any number of passing servants would notice, it being only late afternoon, but he did that, too. He had planned to ask her to leave her door open for him tonight, so it would be entirely her decision. He had simply meant to so heat her with desire today that there would be no other decision for her to make. And he certainly hadn't expected to so dazzle her with one kiss that she was completely his in that moment, to do with as he would.

It was too stirring a kiss, too craved to not be. They were both ignited by it instantly, bodies crushed together, taste and senses exploding in sensual delight. It was her dazed look when he finally let her go that had him picking her up and carrying her upstairs. She had no time to come to her senses. She was still clinging to him when he got her inside her room. Unfortunately, he'd had a little time himself, and a scowling stare from his housekeeper on the way, to jolt him out of his own rashness.

This *wasn't* how he meant to have her. It *wasn't* going to salvage his conscience later, that he had given her no opportunity to think, let alone decide to embrace ruination for a few moments of immense pleasure.

He forced himself to set her down in the middle of her room. He kissed her again, gently now. He waited for her eyes to become focused.

Then cupping her face in his hands, he told her, "You've exhausted yourself today. Take a nap before dinner. I may not join you. I doubt I'd be able to keep my hands off of you long enough to eat. I will join you later, though, if you will leave your door unlocked for me tonight. Follow your heart, Larissa. I promise you pleasure unimagined."

Incredible, to have left her there. If he didn't think himself an utter fool for doing so, he might have been proud of himself . . .

And he made sure that his housekeeper saw him returning downstairs.

Chapter 13

$\mathcal{L}$arissa did indeed take a nap that afternoon. It refreshed her, though it didn't help to clear her confusion over her latest encounter with the baron.

She wasn't sure exactly what had happened between them, or what he had implied would happen. He had sounded like a parent—or a husband—when she had entered the house and he had railed at her for what he considered reckless behavior. And since he had never been either, what was she to think? He cared. It was patently obvious. In the brief time she had known him, he had come to care about her.

And that incredible kiss. She had still been cold, standing there in the entryway. He had warmed her completely. She had still been slightly trembling from it. She had trembled even more from his kiss.

She had never experienced anything even remotely like it. She had left Portsmouth without ever having had any real interest in any young man; thus she'd never let one kiss her. And she had spent her first year in London pouting, which didn't include any socializing, nor was much done in the last two years, other than with her father's business associates.

She had never realized how lacking she was in social congress with young men she might like, let alone be seriously attracted to, as she was to the baron. She had been promised a Season that would most likely find her a husband, and had been perfectly content to wait for it.

She was in no hurry, after all, to leave her family, who were still in need of her. But her father had expected her to marry soon, now that she was of age to do so. Her brother did, too. She had been resigned to it herself, even slightly looking forward to it finally, when the trouble started with her father's business. And now—she was resigned to not having a Season after all.

He cared about her.

She was still having trouble grasping the implications of that, other than that the thought thrilled her. She wasn't quite naive, though, about what he'd meant by not being able to keep his hands off of her, nor about what would likely happen if she did unlock her door tonight.

Her father had found her alone with a young man the year before they'd moved to London. It wasn't what he'd imagined; the fellow was the brother of one of her good friends, and she'd been talking to him about his current romantic interest, who happened to be another of her friends.

But her father had felt compelled to explain to her about men's unruly desires, a most embarrassing conversation for them both, but most enlightening, too, about things she could only have guessed at before.

The baron cared about her *and* he desired her. His remarks had cleared that up for her, where before she never would have believed either of him—which was one reason for her prior confusion. She simply hadn't believed he was interested

147

in her that way—nothing he had said supported it—so the heat she'd seen in his eyes couldn't have been from passion. But it was. She didn't doubt it now. And it had been there almost from the beginning.

Could she marry him, though, after what he had done to her family? He was directly responsible for their losing their home. But it hadn't been personal, had been just another business transaction for him, and of course, he was in a position to make complete amends for it, had already made some by bringing them into his own house.

She could marry him; indeed, that thought thrilled her, too. And it was what he must have in mind. She was of good family, after all. He wouldn't consider making love to her without offering marriage. He had probably just been too overcome with impatience to mention it yet.

She could understand that. She was skirting around his "pleasure unimagined" remark, didn't dare think of that, or she would have been overcome with impatience herself, nearly was already. She was even counting the minutes until she would retire tonight.

She almost didn't go down to dinner. Vincent

had said he wouldn't be there, but if he was, she didn't think she'd get much eating done. But she went, and it was a solitary meal, or at least it was until an unknown gentleman walked in, clearly expecting to find the baron at his meal. His surprise was evident, to find her there in the dining room instead.

"Oh ho, are you for me?" was the first thing he said to her.

He seemed absolutely delighted by that prospect, whatever he meant by it. She wasn't quite sure.

"Excuse me?"

"A sop to keep me happy until Vincent finds what I commissioned him to?"

That didn't clear up the confusion. "I'm afraid I don't know what you're talking about."

He blushed now, apparently realizing he'd made a mistake. "Beg pardon, miss, truly. Lord Hale here. 'Fraid I wasn't expecting to find a lady in this bachelor residence, and one alone—or are you not alone? Here with your father? Never say with a husband?"

She was on firmer ground now. "I'm awaiting my father here."

"Is Vincent a business associate of your father's, then?" he asked.

"No, he recently became our landlord—and evicted us from our house."

She shouldn't have added that. It was certainly none of his business why she was there or how she'd got there, and now she was the one blushing for letting her bitterness over that show.

It also surprised him enough to say, "The devil he did. Kicked you out? So you'd end up here?"

"Well, no, that had nothing to do with it. He's offered us temporary lodging so that he can be assured of speaking with our father when he returns. Some misunderstanding that needs to be straightened out."

"Then your father isn't actually—here? You're here alone?"

"No, my brother is with me, and several of our servants," she replied.

He seemed disappointed by that. "Ah, everything on the up and up, then. Oh well, I'll get over it, I'm sure."

He wasn't making much sense again, but no matter, he seemed harmless enough. He was about the baron's age, not nearly as tall and rather chunky of build, with light blue eyes and a rag-mop of unruly black curls that seemed designed to look so unkempt. He would even be considered handsome if one didn't compare him to the baron, who was too handsome.

Since he didn't seem inclined to leave, simply stood there in the doorway sighing as he gazed at her, she thought to ask, "Did you have an appointment with the baron?"

"Not really, just my weekly check on his progress, though he was probably expecting me, since I show up about this time each week. I'm a bit impatient to receive what he's finding for me."

"Which is?" she asked rather stiffly, thinking he might be the gentleman who had wanted their house so badly that Vincent had bought it out from under them. But then she blushed. "I'm sorry, that was presumptuous of me."

"Not a'tall. It's a painting. A special painting that I simply *must* own for myself. Price is no object. I know, I know, silly of me to put so much stock in possessing something, but there you have it. I'm the first to admit I'm eccentric. And I've run out of things to spend my money on. A deplorable state of affairs. Rather boring, too."

She smiled. She couldn't imagine anyone so rich that it became boring. And as long as he wasn't the fellow who had coveted her home, she had nothing against him, was even grateful to him for taking her mind off of what she expected to happen later tonight.

"I'm sure you'd be welcome to stay for dinner," she offered. "I don't think the baron will be joining us, though. I'm not even sure he's at home just now."

"Oh, he is. The butler wouldn't have let me in the door otherwise. I suppose I should seek him out." Another sigh. "But I'll see you again soon. Depend upon it. Think I might be stopping by daily now for reports. Yes, I just might."

Chapter 14

"*How* much is she going to cost me?"

It took a moment for Vincent to realize that Jonathan Hale wasn't talking about the painting he'd hired Vincent to find for him, which he had been known to refer to as "she," because of its title, *La Nymph*. But only a moment, since he did happen to have been thinking about the same "she" when Jonathan entered his study.

He still asked, "Who?"

"That dazzling wench you've left to dine alone across the hall."

Vincent stiffened. "She isn't for sale."

"Nonsense, everyone has a price."

Trust Jonathan to think so. Vincent had known the viscount long before Jon came to him to find *La Nymph* for him. It was common knowledge among the *ton* that Hale was obscenely rich, which had heretofore made it a simple matter for him to be able to obtain anything his heart desired.

He was used to naming a price and getting what he wanted. That he'd finally found something that he couldn't have was not a matter of the item being unavailable; it had merely not been found as yet. Which was why he had approached Vincent and offered him a ridiculous sum of money merely to locate the painting for him. Jonathan would then negotiate with the current owner himself to buy it.

It was one of the harder commissions that Vincent had accepted. He was more in the habit of barter, of give and get, of finding out what was needed to obtain something, and supplying it. But what he was doing for Jonathan Hale was more or less searching for a rumor.

The actual existence of a painting called *La Nymph* was confirmed, but not the notoriety about it. It was reputed to be of a beautiful young woman so erotically depicted that it had an aphrodisiac effect on anyone gazing upon it, male or female. It was reputed to have kept one of its previous owners, an earl in his seventies, in a constant state of sexual readiness. It had caused marriages to be ruined. It had caused one man to go insane. It had sent another to the poorhouse.

Hearing of all this, Jonathan had decided he *had* to have it in his collection. Whether the painting did what it was reputed to do erotically didn't matter to him, he wanted it because it was so notorious.

Some said *La Nymph* had been commissioned by one of the kings by the name of Henry, that it was of his favorite mistress, but with so many kings of that name, no one had ever figured out which one. Some said it had been created in revenge by the artist, that the young woman in the painting had been his love and had spurned him. Most people who heard about the painting simply didn't believe in its existence. It was a joke. A hoax. Titillating dinner conversation.

Vincent would have been inclined to believe the latter if his search hadn't produced some valid information about the last known owner of the painting. He had been a gambler by the name of Peter Markson who had won a painting called *La Nymph* in a card game several years ago. A lucky stroke for him, since he was apparently not very good at gambling, and in fact had had to leave the country to escape debtor's prison. He'd used the painting to pay for his passage, then was taken ill at sea and died aboard ship.

The captain of that vessel held possession of it next, his name unconfirmed. He didn't keep it long, though, turned it over to the owner of his ship, because after he took it home with him, his wife then threatened to leave him if he didn't get it out of her house.

This was information picked up on the docks, so not really dependable. It made a good tale for seamen to pass about once they heard of the erotic nature of the painting, but was suspect because the names of the ship, its captain, and its owner were never the same twice. Apparently each old salt who wanted to tell the tale made sure it was about a captain or ship he knew or had sailed on.

Yet it was the closest Vincent had come to finding out anything about *La Nymph*. And Peter Markson really did leave the country in disgrace, having lost everything he owned on the turn of a card. That was the only fact that Vincent was inclined to depend on.

As for Jonathan's sudden keen interest in Larissa, that was understandable. She'd had the same effect on Vincent when he'd first seen her, of wanting her at any cost. But with Jonathan, he couldn't take it seriously, because he knew the man's preferences where women were concerned.

So he gave him a thoughtful look and said, "I suppose her price would be marriage."

He had thought that would put Jonathan off, since he was a confirmed bachelor who preferred not to dabble with innocents, when there were so many well-experienced ladies more than willing to entertain him for a pretty bauble or two. And Jon didn't look too happy with the "price."

"Hmmm, hadn't planned to marry," Jonathan complained. "What need when I've all the women I could ask for, and a few carts full of bastards as well to pick an heir from? Marriage never struck me as being a fun thing to do. But I suppose it wouldn't hurt to try it."

That gave Vincent pause. "You aren't serious."

"Why not?"

"For the very reasons you've stated. You've become accustomed to variety in your women. A wife doesn't provide that."

"Mistresses do."

"Then why marry?"

"To have her."

"Then why have mistresses?"

Jonathan frowned. "For the variety—and why are you trying to talk me out of it?"

"Because you merely want to possess her. You have no intention of devoting yourself fully to her. Having come to know her since she has been staying here, I think she deserves better than that in a marriage."

"Or you planned to marry her yourself," Jonathan all but accused.

"No."

Jonathan raised a skeptical brow. "Then you can't object to my courting her. I'll even make my intentions clear, if you insist, that I have no desire to give up my present way of life, merely want to add her to it. All up and up. The truth. Sounds challenging, don't it?"

"You think to sway her with your wealth?"

Jonathan grinned. "Of course."

It was amazing, how strong the urge was to wipe that smile from the viscount's lips with his fist. Emotion again. It was sneaking up on Vincent too much lately, and in fact his emotional outburst today in the hall when Larissa had returned from her errands had quite shocked him later when he had time to reflect on it.

He should have made love to her this afternoon. She'd been willing—at least, she hadn't been objecting. Then this conversation with Hale wouldn't have bothered him very much. He would have been done with her himself, would have accomplished his goal. What matter, then, if Hale courted her or even married her?

The thought still didn't sit well with him. Before, after, it made no difference, he did *not* like the thought of her marrying Jonathan and being merely another acquisition in his vast collection. And she was vulnerable right now. Thinking her father wasn't coming back, that she and her brother were soon going to be without an income, the few valuables she meant to sell unable to support them indefinitely, she just might jump at the chance to marry one of the most wealthy men in the realm, no matter the reasons offered. Vincent had intended to use that same vulnerability to get her into his own bed.

This bloody revenge thing was turning him into someone he didn't much like. A cad, no doubt about it. At least Hale's intentions toward the girl were honorable, if unsavory, while Vincent's were just the opposite.

In a moment of conscience, he said, "Court her by all means, and good luck."

He actually meant it, was thinking only of Larissa's best interests in that moment. He even hoped that she'd had enough time to realize how foolhardy it would be to leave her door unlocked to him tonight, because conscience or not, that was one temptation he knew damn well he wouldn't be able to resist, wouldn't even try.

Chapter 15

$\mathcal{L}$ord Hale kept him longer than expected, chatting about inconsequential things that nearly brought Vincent to rudely show him the door. He restrained himself, just barely, and only because Jonathan was a client. But when Vincent finally got to his room, he was in a state of frustrated impatience that he couldn't seem to control.

He dismissed his valet, tore off his clothes, and donned a robe. Then did nothing. He stood in the middle of his room and stared at the bathroom door, and didn't take a single step toward it.

It was going to be locked, he knew it was, and

he didn't want to find that out for certain. And if it was, he knew he'd be up all night, trying it again and again, in hope that she just hadn't got around to opening it yet, when if it wasn't open by now, it probably wasn't going to get opened at all. Either way, it was going to be a long night.

Everything in him insisted he open that door immediately, yet he was so loath to face the disappointment of it being locked that it was an actual fear. Another emotion she was making him feel . . .

How in the bloody hell had this become so important to him? She was just a lovely conquest, wasn't she? She would be an hour or two of pleasure, no more. She would also be another notch in his campaign of revenge, though that was a point that didn't seem to matter much now, was no more than a sop for his conscience.

He didn't like this hold she had on him, when he didn't understand what it was. The seducer had become the seduced. He wanted her now at any cost and that frightened him. He should leave her be. He should get her out of his house even, put her back in her own if necessary, anything to get her beyond his manipulation. With her here and so accessible, she actually had more control over him than he did her. That had been proven today when she had held his emotions, his every thought, his body, all at her whim. Thank God she was too innocent to know how to use that against him.

Larissa stood there in the bathroom for nearly an hour, staring at the lock on the connecting door. She wasn't going to turn it. Rational thought had prevailed, even though it was making her miserable. She'd marry Vincent, yes, but she must have his proposal first. That was the proper order to go about these things.

But the promised "pleasure unimagined" wouldn't leave her thoughts either, which was why she was still standing there, abject over her decision, and unaware that she was trying to find a way to get around it. Her pulse was racing as she imagined him on the other side of that door, waiting.

Surely he had realized himself by now that a proposal was required before they indulge in any more pleasure of any sort, let alone the kind she was sure he had in mind. He could have intended to ask her tonight, though. She could be denying them both for no good reason.

She unlocked the door. Vincent proved that

he'd been waiting for the sound of it when it opened only seconds later. They stared at each other. Like liquid gold, his eyes were so hot they seared, melting away any last trace of indecision she'd been feeling.

He shrugged out of his robe, left it on the floor there. She was still fully dressed, now uncomfortably so. Yet she was so mesmerized by his golden eyes that she didn't even think to look at him, at all of him, nor was the option there for long, when his hand slipped behind her neck and drew her close to his body.

Their lips met and melded. It was a ravenous kiss, echoing hunger long denied in them both. Her knees buckled, they became so weak, but there was no danger of falling, she was held so tightly to him.

She was so new to this sort of sensual kissing—this was only her second experience of it—yet he was so skillful at it himself, guiding her, prompting when needed, that her inexperience wasn't given any opportunity to interfere. Not that any hesitancy or inadequacies stood a chance of being noticed amidst the pleasure of tasting each other so fully, they became lost in that kiss.

A groan finally broke it—his. She barely noticed, she was so enthralled by what she was feeling. And swiftly she was carried to his bed. Not hers. She didn't notice that yet either. But it wasn't long before she was noticing something quite extraordinary . . .

Had she really thought all pleasure would derive merely from being held and kissed by him, just because it was so nice by itself? But then how could she have known otherwise? His "pleasure unimagined" had been unassociated with anything specific in her mind, because she had no specifics to draw from other than loose generalities. But it became very associated with his hand on her breast.

Spontaneous reactions went off in numerous parts of her body from that simple placement of his palm. Gooseflesh, butterflies, wet heat, and that was only the beginning. He continued to kiss her and catch each little gasp of pleasure that escaped her, and many did as he began the next lesson in sensual touching.

Even the removal of her clothes was an erotic experience, he did it so slowly, with such thorough caressing of each limb and curve exposed. Amazing that if she touched the underside of her knee, she'd feel nothing, yet his fingers there made her shiver. That it was Vincent touching her made all the difference, and such a difference, such a wealth of new sensations to marvel at.

He had her mind and body so consumed with him and the pleasure he was introducing her to that she wasn't sure what made her realize she'd reached the point of no return without hearing what she needed to hear from him. Not that she had the will, or, certainly, the desire, to stop what was happening either way. It would make her pleasure complete, though, to have confirmed what she already took for granted.

The words came out between the gasps, and not very coherently at that. "I thought . . . Shouldn't you . . . There is the question of . . ."

He must have understood what she was trying to say, because he replied, "This isn't the time for important questions that could tie up the tongue."

So misleading, that remark, and yet so reassuring. She assumed that he was talking of asking her to marry him. And she had to agree, after her own garbled speech, that it was rather impossible to put two thoughts together at the moment. Besides, there was no opportunity to say more, when he was distracting her with his kisses again.

His large body covered her gradually, carefully, so as not to alarm her. She was beyond that, comforted instead by his weight, even as the pressure heightened her arousal. He grasped her hands, held on either side of her head. He kissed her deeply as he took possession of her. The pain was so swift, it was there and gone before she really felt it or had time to stiffen against it, and was as soon forgotten in the onslaught of pure sensual delight that followed, of feeling him buried deep within her.

Briefly she thought that was the end of it, that nothing could be better. How naive. Even his "pleasure unimagined" didn't do justice to the incredible bliss that steadily grew as he began moving in her, then burst and spread through her body in unrelenting waves.

In those few moments of utter ecstasy, nothing else mattered. They would work out the marriage arrangements later, she was sure. For now, she savored the knowledge that Vincent Everett belonged to her.

Chapter 16

The proposal of marriage didn't come after the lovemaking as expected. Not surprising, though, when Vincent removed his weight from Larissa, pulled her close to his side, and promptly fell asleep. And she lay there too, long savoring the whole experience, the happiness she was feeling, and the unexpected comfort of being held by him even in sleep to consider waking him now when she finally realized that part of the evening's agenda hadn't been finished.

She wasn't worried about it, though. Taking things for granted had a way of removing doubts and leaving room only for positive thoughts. She knew she couldn't stay there in his room to sleep the night with him, much as she would have liked to, but had that to look forward to when they married. And before the comfort of his closeness put her to sleep as well, she carefully got out of bed, gathered up her clothes so she'd leave no trace of herself there for any servants to find, and tiptoed back to her room.

She didn't lock the doors between their rooms, didn't even think to. Nor was there a need to now. Making love with Vincent changed so many things, not just her outlook or her future, which was now secure. *She* was changed, and she felt confident in the intimate knowledge she had gained. And she eventually fell asleep with a smile on her lips.

It annoyed Vincent that Larissa wasn't in his bed when he awoke the next morning. He knew it shouldn't, knew she'd been right to leave, would have taken her back to her room himself if he hadn't fallen asleep. Thus his annoyance made no bloody sense in his mind.

And his mood only got worse. Every little thing annoyed him that morning as he dealt with his secretary and his staff. He found himself snapping at the lot of them, and for no good reason.

Unfortunately, that mood didn't leave him before luncheon, and when he joined Larissa in the dining room, he ended up snapping at her as well, before he could stop himself. "My cook is threatening to quit if *your* cook does not stay out of his kitchen!"

He'd all but shouted it, and managed to shock them both. That was certainly not how he'd meant to greet her, and definitely not how he *should* have greeted her, when this was the first time he was seeing her after stealing her virginity last night. It didn't matter that one thing after another this morning had conspired to cause him boundless frustration—and that was just another excuse.

He knew why he was a fuse already lit, he just hadn't owned up to it yet. And he was furious with himself for cowardly refusing to examine the root of his annoyance, and instead taking it out on others—even her.

He was feeling an incredible amount of guilt over what he'd done last night. He'd never in his life enjoyed anything so much, yet now was overcome with regret for it. Because he had no intention of marrying her, when he knew that was what she was expecting from him now.

The original motive of revenge wasn't helping to ease his conscience at all in the matter of his becoming her lover, when he had counted on it doing so. The only thing that might help now was to not let it ruin her reputation as he'd planned to. As long as it didn't become public knowledge, she could still find a good marriage.

He didn't doubt that Hale would marry her either way. He was smitten by her beauty, could care less whether she was a virgin. But could he stomach watching another man pursue her, when just speaking of it last night, he'd wanted to punch the man in the face?

Larissa recovered first from his outburst, explained calmly, "I'm sorry. When I told Mary this morning that we would be living here permanently now, she no doubt decided she could make herself more at home here, and she feels most at home in a kitchen."

Vincent flushed. And he couldn't correct her about living there permanently—not yet. His silence on the matter would confirm it in her mind, but that couldn't be helped. He still expected her father to show up, even if she didn't. And when Ascot did, then Vincent could be done with this bloody business of revenge, deliver the final blow to the man, and then get on with his own life.

He mumbled something about their both keeping their servants in line, and hoped she'd leave it go at that. She did. She even smiled at him, which had the effect of making it worse. He couldn't leave it go himself now. She was such a sweet, gullible chit, and he'd been an absolute bastard in his dealings with her from the start— and was still going to be. The least he could do was make her happy in the meantime, and keep his foul moods to himself.

He moved around the table to her side. He would have kissed her if they were alone, but there were servants entering and leaving, so he merely bent down and whispered to her, "Forgive me for that boorish greeting. And thank you for the most wonderful gift I've ever received."

"What gift?"

"You."

He could feel the heat of her blush, though he was standing behind her and couldn't see it. Her cheeks were still pink when he took his seat across from her and gazed at her. But he detected the barest trace of a smile, proving it wasn't embarrassment making her cheeks glow.

The meal progressed. She chatted aimlessly merely to fill the silence, nothing of import, merely relaxed conversation that he found himself enjoying. She could be amusing when she wasn't nervous, and she wasn't the least bit nervous with him at the moment.

But then she mentioned the Christmas decorations again. He'd already had them fetched. He could just tell her that and nothing more. But this was too ideal an opportunity to mention that the rest of her stored valuables were gone, not when she was requesting them, but while she assumed she wouldn't have to sell them now, so the loss wouldn't hit her so hard. They'd be "found," of course, after her father returned. Vincent had no intention of stealing anything from the Ascots, other than their good reputation.

He didn't consider dispensing with the theft story. He'd already seduced her, yes, but now he had to worry that she would ask him directly about marriage, and if she did, he wasn't going to lie about it. Which would put her back to thinking she had to leave, which he still wasn't willing to let her do. When her father returned would be soon enough to give her up. So having her think she had no means to leave would still be beneficial— for him.

To that end, he managed a suitably grave expression before saying, "Speaking of those Christmas decorations, they arrived here this morning, but I'm afraid some bad news was delivered with them."

"They've been damaged?" she asked in alarm.

"Not that I'm aware of," he quickly assured her. "But apparently there was a robbery late last night at the warehouse where your belongings were stored. The report from the attendant who keeps a watch on the place was that it was a selective robbery, which isn't uncommon, since it can be accomplished in the least amount of time."

"I've been robbed?" she said incredulously.

"*We* have been robbed," he clarified. "I had a few valuables stored there myself. But most of your possessions are still there. As I said, the thieves were selective. They took only what they considered valuable and easily movable, paintings, vases, and other small pieces of art. They were in and gone in under ten minutes, which was the amount of time the attendant was indisposed."

"I had plans for those paintings," she said in a forlorn whisper.

He hadn't counted on her stricken look. He now knew exactly how his secretary had felt that night when she'd turned this look on him. Vincent didn't have the luxury of resigning from what he'd started, however, without admitting he was a despicable liar.

He could, however, lessen the blow, and assured her, "I'm not writing this off, Larissa. The robbery has been reported to the authorities, but I've already assigned my own people to track down these culprits. What was taken *will* be recovered. If your portion isn't found by the beginning of the New Year, I will replace the value myself."

"You . . . don't have to do that," she replied. "It's not your fault—"

He didn't let her finish. "I disagree. It was my warehouse, after all, and I should have had it protected better. I'm afraid I'm not used to owning it yet, and frankly, I wasn't planning to keep it, just haven't got around to disposing of it yet."

"Then why did you buy it?"

He relaxed. Her expression was merely curious now, the horror gone from it. He'd managed to ease her mind and accomplish his goal, and all because she didn't have a suspicious bone in her pretty little body.

"I didn't buy it. It came into my possession a few months ago, was the last asset from my brother's business that didn't succumb to his creditors when he died."

"Oh, I'm so sorry."

Bloody hell, there it was again, sympathy for him pouring out of her. She'd just been delivered a devastating blow, yet had room to feel compassion for him as she realized what he'd said meant his brother had only recently died.

He quickly made light of it in offering her a shrug and a slight change of subject. "Have you no other assets at all, aside from your jewels?"

"There is a piece of land in Kent that's been in my family's possession longer than anyone can remember. There is a ruined castle on it, believed to have belonged to one of our ancestors, an ancient one. But that rumor has never been confirmed. Unfortunately, it only takes one generation to go by, uninterested in preserving family history, for that history to be lost."

"The land is valuable, though?"

"I suppose it is, but I can't sell it. My father hasn't been declared dead yet, for me to be able to. The same goes for his company, his ships, any stored cargoes or valuables he has locked in the small storeroom at the company, none of which I can dispose of yet. And his personal belongings, jewelry and the like, sailed with him."

Vincent stiffened. Talk of ships in relation to her father brought a very unacceptable—to him— thought.

It hadn't occurred to him, until that moment, that Larissa's father fit the description of the current possessor of *La Nymph*, and that she had paintings she meant to sell . . . No, that would be too easy, too convenient—and make her family incredibly rich. But just in case it wasn't a coincidence, he would visit the warehouse after luncheon to examine those paintings himself that had been moved to the secured storeroom in the back of the building. And he hoped, he really did, that he wouldn't find *La Nymph* there.

Chapter 17

$\mathcal{V}$incent returned to his house in a much better mood than he'd been in upon leaving it. The trip to the warehouse showed that the Ascots were in possession of seven old paintings, two by well-known artists, but none of them the notorious *La Nymph* that he was searching for. So he didn't have to face the dilemma of making the Ascots very rich, something that just did *not* fit into his plans for their ruination.

And then he had his mood utterly ruined again by finding Jonathan Hale in his parlor with Larissa and her brother, Thomas, who'd been allowed out of the sickroom for the express purpose of decorating the Christmas tree. Such a homey scene, and so foreign to him.

It was the laughter and smiles, the sheer enjoyment they were having, that hit Vincent the worst. He wasn't part of it, nor ever would be. And it wasn't even strictly related to Christmas, though that was the present reason for it. They simply knew how to have fun doing simple things, while the concept of fun had never been part of his own life, even as a child.

More than once his brother had tried to show him how to have fun, would drag him from his studies, explain some imaginary game, then be disappointed when Vincent couldn't get the hang of it. There were simply too many real concerns always plaguing Vincent as a child for him to let go of them long enough to have fun. But that Albert had tried to include him in that aspect of life was one reason he had tolerated his brother's many weaknesses throughout the years. Albert had tried to teach him. Vincent hadn't really tried to learn.

Larissa noticed him standing there in the doorway and gave him a brilliant smile. She took his breath away, she was so incredibly beautiful.

Jonathan saw it as well and stood there mesmerized. Thomas, noticing both men, rolled his eyes
toward the ceiling. Obviously he was used to men
behaving like idiots around his sister.

"I didn't think you would return in time to
help," she told Vincent, motioning him forward.

He didn't move. "Help?"

"It's your tree, really. Our decorations are only
being added to the contributions your servants
have already made. Look at this one from your
grouchy cook." She pointed out a small shiny
spoon that had a hole punched in the end of it so
it could be tied to a branch with a bright ribbon.
"He even blushed as he put it on."

"I have no decorations to add."

"There are plenty here to choose from. Come,
put this angel on the top."

There was a sturdy chair placed next to the tree,
to use to reach the upper branches. Vincent simply
couldn't picture himself standing on it, yet he
found himself walking forward. *She* was the draw,
not the silly tree, which had no business being inside a house.

He took the ornament from her, glanced at the
top of the tree, which was a good three feet above

his head. He stood on the chair. She stood behind it, holding the back to keep it steady for him. He looked down at her, caught his breath yet again. She looked so delighted. It was too easy to make her happy. She took joy in such little things.

He placed the angel on the top of the tree. Not correctly, apparently, since she began to direct him to try again, and again. Hale started making jokes about angels becoming fallen in his hands, which fortunately, Larissa saw no double meaning in, but Vincent certainly did.

Finally she clapped and said, "Perfect!"

Thomas, standing across the room to view it from a different angle, said, "It's crooked."

"Bah, don't listen to him, Vince, he's being ornery."

Hale chimed in, "Crooked."

"See? Majority rules." Thomas chuckled.

"You don't have a majority yet without my vote," Vincent heard himself saying.

"Well, then, what's the verdict?"

Vincent stepped off the chair, moved about the room looking at the tree from different directions, keeping them waiting while he seemed to give it serious thought. Finally he stopped next to

Thomas and said, "Crooked. You fix it. I obviously don't have a knack for it," and he lifted Thomas up to straighten the ornament, which he did.

Across the room, Larissa pealed with laughter. "Now it's crooked."

It was infectious this time, her laughter. Vincent heard himself joining in with the others and was amazed at how good it felt. He sat back after that and watched them finish, making a comment here or there, pointing out a few barren spots on the tree that could use some help.

He still couldn't quite believe that he had joined their festive group and actually felt a part of it. But then that was Larissa's doing. It wasn't that she had a knack for taking command, was more that people simply wanted to please her by doing whatever she requested of them.

Vincent couldn't *not* invite Hale to dinner after all his help, much as he would have preferred it otherwise. While the child had been present in the parlor, Hale had been the perfect gentleman, merely part of the group. But now with the boy sent back to his bed, Hale turned every bit of charm he could muster in Larissa's direction.

Vincent was disgusted. He would have said

something to warn Jonathan to back off, but Larissa was doing too good a job of evading, and for the most part, ignoring or simply not understanding some of the more subtle overtures coming her way. And he realized, after a while, that he had nothing to worry about.

For the time being, and until she learned the truth, she considered herself soon to be married, which meant she would ignore any offerings from other men. Yet because Vincent hadn't asked her to marry him yet, she couldn't use that as an excuse to refuse invitations from others; she had to be creative in her turndowns instead.

She was doing an admirable job of that, much to Jonathan's chagrin. Yet she did it in such a way that Hale didn't lose hope, much to Vincent's chagrin. He would have preferred the man go away and not come back. No such luck, he was sure. And he did notice, when she declined going to the theater, that she seemed rather disappointed to have to refuse.

He wondered then if she had ever been to the theater before, and rather doubted it. Reclusive, she had been, from all accounts, and unknown to the *ton*. Her father could have taken her, but she had only just come of age, and taking her prior to that would have been inappropriate.

He decided to invite her himself, when he joined her later tonight. A small thing that might give her a lot of enjoyment. The least he could do, and besides, it might distract her from asking pertinent questions that he needed to continue to avoid himself.

Chapter 18

$\mathcal{A}$s a distraction, inviting Larissa to the theater worked wonders. She had intended to address the issue of marriage that night when Vincent joined her in her room. That had been fairly obvious by her nervousness. And she even began the question he didn't want to hear.

But having expected it—since he was quite aware that while they were alone was really the only chance she would have to bring up anything that personal— he was swift in cutting her off with the invitation. And before they were done discussing the particulars of him taking her on such an excursion, he was kissing her. And of course, once that began, there were no further thoughts about anything other than the pleasure to come.

The guilt was still there and bothering him, but it didn't stop Vincent from making love to Larissa again that night. *That* was a compulsion that far outweighed any remorse he might be feeling. And his conscience did seem to absent itself nicely once he gathered her in his arms. It was only later, when she wasn't near him, that the guilt would set in to bedevil him again.

He avoided her the next day up until it was time to leave. She had claimed that she had appropriate clothes for such an outing, since her Season wardrobe had been made long before the new Season began. He had cautioned her against anything too fancy, and she had complied. The clothes did determine which theater they would go to, after all, and there were many to choose from, the more esteemed establishments frequented by the *ton* to the common variety that one might find a chimney sweep standing in line for.

She had done exactly as he'd asked. Her rose

velvet gown could have been worn for day wear with the short, fur-trimmed cape covering the deep scoop of the neckline. But once the cape was removed, the gown was definitely evening wear, and definitely too elegant for a theater frequented by the lower masses.

One of her servants accompanied them. Chaperonage was good, in his opinion. It kept him from touching Larissa, kept him from seeming the least bit proprietary—kept him from ravaging her in the coach on the way to the theater district, which might have been a definite possibility, as lovely as she looked that night.

It turned out to be a complete blunder on his part, however, to take her anywhere where she would be *seen*. She enjoyed it immensely, yes, but he could have found some other way to amuse her.

The results began the next morning. No fewer than seven young dandies showed up at his door to call on the young beauty they had glimpsed with him last evening. And worse, he wasn't there to fend them off, had gone on his morning ride in the park. By the time he returned home, Larissa was holding court in his parlor, next to her Christmas tree. And the parade of young bucks continued that afternoon with another five gentlemen calling.

The only thing that Vincent was able to console himself with was that Larissa was still declining all invitations. How much longer that would last, though, when she didn't have an actual verbal commitment from him yet, was the burning question he had to deal with.

She was his on borrowed time. When her father showed up, she wouldn't be his any longer. And unlike her, *he* didn't expect that time to continue more than a few more days. Which was the only reason his current evasive tactics were going to work. Her question couldn't be put off indefinitely, when it was too important to her to get an answer. And he was sure she would like to be able to say officially, "I'm engaged, leave me alone," to all her new admirers.

When Lord Hale showed up that evening, he had already heard about the excursion. Not surprisingly, he was quite put out with Vincent for introducing Larissa to the *ton*.

Jonathan even went so far as to accuse him, "You've already asked her to marry you and been accepted, haven't you? You're just waiting for her father to return to England to make it official. 'Fess up, Vincent. I'm wasting my bloody time here, aren't I?"

"What, pray tell, does the one have to do with the other?" Vincent asked him.

"You wouldn't feel confident in showing her off unless you already had her committed to you. Or are you going to try to tell me that you didn't know you'd have half the *ton* knocking at your door after they got a look at her? Now, I know you well enough to know that you don't like to entertain here. So what does that leave in assumptions, eh? That you couldn't resist showing her off, just as I'd planned to do *after* I got her committed to me. I'm not fool enough to do it beforehand, and neither are you."

Vincent only just managed to resist laughing. Should he 'fess up to being the fool Hale had just described? He really hadn't thought of the repercussions that would result from taking Larissa out for an evening's entertainment. He had wanted to distract her. He had wanted to offer her some amusement, nothing more.

And he *had* tried to avoid the *ton* by going to a less prestigious theater, but only so he wouldn't have to fend off questions about her from acquaintances they might run into. That had back-fired, of course, due to the play in question having received excellent reviews, which he hadn't been aware of, which was a sure draw for the theater-frequenting crowd, including those from his social circle. But then, unlike Hale, he wasn't hoping to marry Larissa, so wasn't thinking about keeping other men from noticing her.

They had gathered in the parlor after dinner. Larissa had just excused herself to retire. It had been a strenuous day for her, apparently, being ad-mired by so many.

Hale was obviously disappointed to see her go—he had arrived late himself and so hadn't had a chance to spend much time with her today. That might account for half of his annoyance.

"I believe I've already mentioned to you that I have no plans to marry Larissa or anyone else for that matter," Vincent said.

"You have eyes. The girl is nigh impossible to resist."

"Nonsense," Vincent maintained, and even man-aged to keep a straight face doing so. "She's beau-tiful, yes, but I have no desire to complicate my life with a wife."

"You'll need to marry sometime."

"Why? You hadn't planned to, prior to meeting Larissa. Nor do I require an heir."

"You've a title to bestow," Jonathan pointed out.

"My title can rot. I have nothing I care to leave to anyone."

"That ain't normal, Vincent."

Vincent shrugged to show how little he cared for normality, though he did add, "Besides, this is redundant. I have not asked the girl to marry me, nor will I. As to your concern over my taking her to the theater, did it not occur to you that I might have simply wanted to distract the girl from her worries? Or weren't you aware that her father's tardiness has her assuming the worst? And besides, I *thought* I was taking her to a play that wouldn't be frequented by our crowd. Bloody ill luck that it was such a good performance that word of it has spread."

"Her father could be dead?"

Trust Jonathan to surmise that and be already thinking how to put that information to good use in his campaign to win her. "Highly unlikely."

"But possible?"

"Anything is possible, of course. But it's more

likely that he will show up within the week, that whatever has detained him, he will make an effort to finish up. He will want to be home for Christmas, after all, to spend it with his family. Larissa, unfortunately, has it set in her mind that something has gone terribly wrong, and once a fear sets in, it's hard to shake. I've tried to convince her otherwise, with little luck. So I tried a distraction instead."

Jonathan frowned. "She hides it very well, that she's worried. How did you find out?"

"Having her burst into tears in front of me when we had been speaking of her father was a very good clue," Vincent said dryly.

"I would be quite happy to take over the matter of distracting her. No reason for you to be bothered, when she means nothing to you. And you've already done quite enough in allowing the girl and her brother to stay here until their father returns. Which reminds me, why *did* you evict them from their home?"

Jonathan was overstepping the bounds of their relationship in asking questions that were none of his business. He knew that, of course. His slight blush said as much. Yet he wasn't going to retract the question, because his interest in Larissa naturally included all information he could gather about her, and he no doubt hoped Vincent would realize that and supply some of it.

Vincent sighed. It wasn't his habit to lie, yet he seemed to be doing a great deal of it since he'd met Larissa. And having assured Jonathan that he had no interest in the girl himself, he couldn't very well tell the viscount that she'd been brought into his home so he could seduce her, nor that his goal was to ruin her family's good name. That would be information Hale would relish sharing with Larissa, if for no other reason than he'd expect her to be grateful.

So he found himself continuing the lie he'd already begun with her. "It was a business decision carried out before I was aware that George Ascot wasn't in the country and so unavailable to move his family elsewhere. When it did come to my attention that his children would be left homeless and without guidance, I brought them here to await his return."

"Ah, well, glad to hear you aren't completely heartless," Jonathan replied.

Vincent frowned, remarking, "Not to say I admit to having a heart in that context, but just what was heartless about my actions?"

"Evicting them during the holidays," Jonathan clarified. "Rather harsh, that."

"Bah, just what do the holidays have to do with conducting business as usual?"

Jonathan blinked. "Well, actually, nothing, now you mention it. It's just that this particular holiday is synonymous with generosity and goodwill."

"Sorry, but unlike you, I have no sentimentality toward this holiday, nor any preconceived notions about it. For me it's just another day."

"Now, that's sad, Vincent."

"Why?"

"Because you've obviously never experienced the joy and cheer that go along with the generosity and goodwill. Quite uplifting, if I do say so myself. Enemies call truce. Neighbors remember they have neighbors. You find good cheer and well-wishes everywhere you look. You can't say you've never experienced any of that."

Vincent shrugged. "Not that I recall."

"Bloody hell, I thought you were English," Jonathan grumbled, which caused Vincent to burst out laughing and the viscount to demand, "What's so funny?"

"Just that Larissa assumed the same thing, when I mentioned I'd never had a Christmas tree before."

"So this one here that *you* helped to decorate is just for her?" Jonathan snorted before he got an answer. "For someone who's never experienced the generosity of the season, you're being damned generous where that chit is concerned. A word of advice, then. You might want to tone that down a bit, or *she* might get the idea that you're interested in her, when, as you say, you aren't."

Chapter 19

*A*ssumptions had a way of easing doubts, but they also crumbled when subjected to too much time and scrutiny. Such was the case for Larissa. And after a bit more than a week had gone by since the night she had succumbed to temptation, she finally had to conclude that if Vincent was going to ask her to marry him, he would have done so by now. Which meant he wasn't going to.

Oddly enough, she wasn't devastated by that conclusion. But then he hadn't broken any promise to her. He hadn't deceived her in any way. She had done that to herself with her silly assumptions.

He had been as much a victim as she of the powerful attraction between them. The end results just didn't equal the same thing for them both. She had naturally thought marriage, being a romantic at heart, while he apparently simply took his pleasure where he found it. She couldn't blame him for that. She figured it was as natural for him to do as it was for her to have expected more.

She supposed it might have hit her much worse, that he didn't want to make their relationship permanent, if she weren't already grieving over her father and what his absence meant. Ironically, she knew she had Vincent to thank for keeping her mind off of that grief.

Night after night he had come to her room. It had been addicting, his lovemaking. She had waited in breathless anticipation for his touch each night. All of which had added benefits for her that he certainly wasn't aware of, because when she was with him, she thought only of him, but when she wasn't, her grief would set in again.

She had no longer been able to hide that grief from her astute brother either. Which was why Thomas no longer asked her when their father was coming home. And she had caught Thomas crying the day he finally realized that their father wasn't coming home. But by silent agreement, they weren't going to speak of it—not yet.

So she had much to be grateful to Vincent for, not just for giving them a home for the holiday, but for his many and varied distractions when she might otherwise have wallowed in complete despair.

She still locked her door again that night, the night before Christmas. She might be grateful to Vincent, but she couldn't continue to have an intimate relationship with him, now that she knew that was all he wanted from her.

It wasn't easy, though. It should have been. She was rather numb, after all, over the new conclusions she'd drawn. But he came as usual, softly called her name from the other side of the locked door. She didn't answer. And she knew she had tried to deceive herself again, because it was hurting more than she'd thought, that he didn't care about her as much as she'd hoped.

The tears that soaked her pillow that night were for what might have been . . .

For Thomas's sake, Larissa wore a bright, cheerful expression as she woke him and dragged him down to the parlor to open his presents, which she had bought and had hidden away many months ago. He had tucked a few under the tree for her as well, when she wasn't looking, carvings he had made himself, and some for Mara and Mary, who joined them for the fun of present opening.

Of course, it wasn't a normal Christmas for them. It wasn't their house, wasn't even their tree that they'd put presents under. But that had nothing to do with giving. Christmas wasn't about a place, after all; for them it was about family, and sharing, and love. And that was where it wasn't normal, since they weren't a complete family this Christmas and were sore missing that completeness on such a traditional day of gathering together.

Mara and Mary helped them to forget, ohing and ahing over Thomas's whittling skill, which was improving each year, and over the little trinkets Larissa gave them, which, fortunately, she had bought before the money ran out. Mary didn't stay long, though, anxious to get to the kitchen, which was Larissa's real gift to her, having talked Vincent's cook into letting Mary cook the Christmas goose for dinner, which she did so well.

She didn't worry about Thomas getting over-excited either, as he tended to do on Christmas, though she would have a week ago. But he was recovered from his sickness finally, thank God, not quite as full of energy yet, but much more his usual buoyant self.

"May I have a word alone with your sister?"

Vincent stood in the open doorway. He looked a bit hesitant to enter the room.

Thomas, to whom the question had been addressed, didn't glance his way, nor was there any inflection in his voice when he replied, "Not if you're going to make her cry again."

"Excuse me?" Stiffness now.

"Her eyes are all red—"

"Thomas, hush!" Larissa cut in, thoroughly embarrassed by now. "That has nothing to do with him," she added, and blushed a bit more for the lie. "Please, take your new soldiers and go upstairs. I'll join you shortly."

Thomas gave her a disgusted look that indicated he knew very well she was lying. But Mara, much more tactful, helped him gather his new wooden soldiers and books, and half prodded, half dragged him out of the room.

Vincent wasn't nearly as astute, or deliberately chose not to be, because as soon as they were alone, he said, "You were crying over your father again?"

"No."

He blushed now. Well, if he hadn't wanted the truth, he shouldn't have asked a question that would lead to it. And she didn't take pity on him. It was time for plain speaking between them. He had repeatedly avoided or evaded her questions when they were alone at night, and in the day there was never the opportunity to speak of anything personal with so many servants always near to hand. But for once they were alone, and he wasn't kissing her to distraction or cutting her off with silly remarks until he *could* kiss her to distraction. In fact, for once, he was the one with burning questions.

"Why wouldn't you answer me last night?"

"Probably for the same reason you never answer me," she replied.

"What are you talking about?"

She gave him a sad smile. "Come now, Vincent, obtuseness doesn't become you. Anytime I ever begin to mention marriage in your presence, you pounce on another subject so swiftly, I don't even have time to blink. Very well, so marriage is a subject we will never discuss. And now that I've come to realize that, it is rather obvious, isn't it, why my door will henceforth remain locked?"

He frowned. He also started to approach her. She quickly held up a hand, even took several steps back.

Letting him touch her was out of the question, not because it was out in the open now, that he had no intention of marrying her, but because she was too malleable in his arms. But oh God, why didn't the knowledge she now possessed stop her from wanting him? She should despise him— again. She shouldn't be wishing fervently that he would deny it and assure her that yes, of course they would marry.

"You don't really want to do this to us, Larissa, do you?"

His tactics were on the rise, and he had many that he knew would work, including that husky tone he'd just used. How was she going to survive this?

"I don't, but you do. Whether we continue as we were, or we say good-bye today, is entirely up to you. I can only follow my heart."

"Your heart isn't telling you to shut me out."

No, it wasn't. She hadn't realized she had fallen so deeply in love with him. She had begun this only thinking it would be nice to marry him. She hadn't thought why it would be so nice. But all the little things she knew about him had gotten to her, first to her compassion, then into her heart. The overwhelming attraction she felt for him was merely a side benefit—or a curse.

She tried to point out what he seemed to be missing. "Temptation is a lure of the forbidden. By all that's right, you are forbidden to me. Preference has no bearing. If it were just me, if I had no others that I am responsible for, then it might not matter so much. But I have a young brother to raise now—on my own. And he will be taught by example, just as my father would have taught him, the correct path."

"Your father wouldn't have been a good— Never mind." He cut himself off.

He raked a hand through his black mane. His frustration was evident and mounting. Or was it anger? It was hard to tell with him, when he so rarely showed any emotion—other than passion.

She didn't doubt for a minute that he liked their current relationship and wanted it to continue.

The emotion he was displaying was because he didn't want her to end it. But she had no choice. He might care for her, but not enough to want to make her a permanent part of his life. And what did that leave her? What exactly had he envisioned for her? Being his mistress, when her upbringing simply wouldn't allow it? Or had he envisioned no more than a brief love affair that was ending sooner than he'd expected?

She was starting to feel some frustration herself, which was welcome, really. Anything to distract her from the pain squeezing at her heart.

"Vincent, I don't know what you want from me. Do you even know?"

"I know I don't want you to leave me."

"Only marriage would assure that."

"Blast it," he exploded. "I *can't* marry you."

She frowned. "Why not?"

"Because of your father."

Confusion filled her, and with it, alarm. "What about him?"

"There are things you don't know."

"Then tell me!"

"You revere him, Larissa," he replied. "It's better if you don't know."

She paled, drawing her own conclusions yet again. "He *is* dead, isn't he? And you've known all along. You've received proof—"

"No!" He pounced this time, before she could step back again, but only to grab her shoulders. He shook her once. "No, it's nothing like that. Ah, bloody hell, it's not worth it anymore. *You're* more important. But your father is only detained. There's no reason to assume the worst. In fact, I wouldn't be surprised if he showed up today at my door—"

The knock at the front door was too loud to miss hearing, and too prophetic not to strongly affect Larissa. She went utterly still. She held her breath in hopeful anticipation. But it was too much anticipation to wait. She broke out of Vincent's hold, heard him sigh, but ignored it. She ran to the open doorway of the parlor, stared as his butler rushed to deal with the loud visitor.

"I didn't mean he would literally show up this minute, Larissa," Vincent said behind her in a voice that was already starting to reveal sympathy.

She ignored him again, wouldn't listen to denials anymore. This was her *last* hope. Dear God, let it be her father. She'd never ask for another thing, never . . .

It wasn't her father. It was a big, burly man standing there, asking if this was where the Baron of Windsmoor lived. She didn't hear any more after that. A ringing began in her ears. Her vision blurred. She grasped the fact that she was fainting and almost laughed, because she was made of sterner stuff than that. Wasn't she? She had probably just held her breath too long . . .

Vincent caught her before her legs completely buckled. She heard him calling her name, trying to keep her there when her mind was insisting on the oblivion of nothingness. He sounded like her father. Stupid mind playing tricks on her now. He demanded she open her eyes. No, she didn't want to. No more disappointments. She'd had too many.

"Rissa, please, just look at me."

Vincent had never called her Rissa. She opened her eyes, then forgot to breathe again.

"Papa?" she whispered. "Is that really you?"

For an answer, she was pulled into an old, familiar embrace, one of warmth, comfort and love, and everything-will-be-fine-now, an embrace she had grown up depending on. It was he. Oh, God, it was he, alive, and home, and alive, alive . . .

Great, racking sobs of emotion overcame her. She couldn't help it. Her prayers had been answered. The season of miracles had given her one.

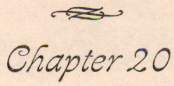

Chapter 20

"Why are my children here?"

It was the first thing George Ascot said to Vincent once they were alone. He was a big, heavyset man in his middle years. His light brown hair had a bit of gray at the temples; the trimmed beard had much more. His eyes were disconcertingly the exact shade of blue-green as Larissa's, with that same warmth indicative of a compassionate nature, falsely so in his case, of course.

Vincent had stood there silently and watched the tearful reunion, witnessed the love and tenderness pouring out of the father for the daughter, which had somewhat surprised him. But what had he expected? Just because the man dealt viciously with his competitors didn't mean he couldn't love his family. Even a devil could love his children if he had any and be no less evil, he supposed.

Larissa shouldn't have left them alone. She had finished her crying, and finally her laughing, and had run upstairs to fetch her brother to give him the good news. She hadn't even asked yet what had detained her father. That wasn't very important to her apparently, now that he was safe and sound—and home.

Vincent could have offered the man excuses. He could have made amends as well. If she hadn't left them alone, he might have, for he'd already decided that his revenge wasn't worth losing her. An amazing discovery which she had only just forced him to realize. But as he stood there alone in the hall with the man responsible for his brother's death, the feelings returned that started it all. And unfortunately, those feelings governed his response.

"You left them without guidance or wherewithal; they had nowhere else to go," Vincent said.

George would have had to be deaf to miss the disgust in Vincent's tone, and although he didn't understand it yet, he still took offense, replying stiffly, "Rissa had ample household funds."

"When there were panicked creditors hounding her to settle accounts?"

"Panicked? What could possibly—?"

"Rumors that your underhanded business practices led you to financial ruin perhaps?"

"Preposterous!"

Vincent shrugged, unimpressed with the man's florid-faced indignation. "You weren't here to prove otherwise, were you? In fact, your prolonged absence only confirmed and strengthened the suspicions that you weren't planning on returning to England at all."

"My family was still here! No one in their right mind would conclude that I would abandon them!"

"Someone without ethics wouldn't worry about throwing his family to the wolves. It happens all the time. Besides, how were your creditors to know that your family wasn't already making plans to abandon England as well?"

George became infused with even more indignant color. "You sound as if you believe those ridiculous rumors."

"Perhaps because I do."

"Why? You don't even know me."

"Don't I? Did you not learn my name before you sent your driver pounding on my door?"

George frowned at that point, explaining, "I come home to find my house empty of my family and all furnishings. My nearest neighbors inform me that I can find my family, at least, at Baron Windsmoor's residence and give me the address Rissa left with them. No, actually, I got no more than your title before I hied it here in all haste. Is your name relevant? Just who are you, sir?"

"Vincent Everett."

"Good God, you aren't related to that blackguard Albert Everett, are you?"

Vincent stiffened now. "My brother, now referred to as deceased."

"He's dead?" George asked in surprise. "I'm sorry, I didn't know."

"Don't be a hypocrite, Ascot," Vincent said in disgust. "Sorrow from the man who drove him to his death just doesn't smack of sincerity."

"Drove him—!" George gasped. "What madness are you spouting now?"

"So now you would claim ignorance? Very well,

let me refresh your memory, then. Albert used what little was left of his inheritance to start a business that would support him. Unfortunately, he picked your line of business, and you went out of your way to make sure that he knew the added competition wasn't welcome."

"That isn't—"

"Let me finish," Vincent interrupted. "You undermined his efforts at every turn, had your captains escalate the bids on the cargoes he was after, so he couldn't hope to make a profit on them. You made sure his business would fail, and so it did. You crushed my brother thoroughly, so much so that he killed himself rather than admit to me that he had lost everything. You didn't really think his family would let you get away with that, did you, Ascot?"

The indignation was gone. The older man was red-faced with fury now, though his voice managed to remain calm as he replied, "You have that a bit backwards, sir. If your brother's business failed, it was because he was buying cargoes—*my* cargoes, already contracted to me—at ridiculously high prices, so he was unable to sell them at even close to a return on the investment. I had assumed he had an unlimited supply of funds to do this, which is why I gave up trying to regain the markets he was stealing from me, and sailed west to find new markets. I hadn't heard that he failed, or I wouldn't have left."

"So you're saying that Albert tried to drive you to ruin, and ruined himself in the process?"

"Exactly."

"That's rather convenient, you'll agree, an easy claim to make against a man who can't step forward to deny it, because he's dead."

"The truth is not always easy to swallow, sir, though it can usually be verified. You have only to question my captains, or perhaps the merchants involved, who ignored valid contracts with me to reap quick profits from your brother. These cargoes weren't on the open market to be bid upon as you mentioned, they had set prices already agreed upon. Or perhaps question your brother's own captains, who can tell you that their orders were to obtain cargoes at any costs. Now, whether his captains acted on their own or under his direction, the results were the same. They followed my ships specifically, showing up in all the same ports."

"So now you would put the blame on his captains?" Vincent said.

George sighed. "Actually, I put the blame where it belongs, on your brother. I spoke to him before I left England, to try to find out why he was throwing away good money on underhanded tactics, rather than put a little effort into finding new markets for himself where he could have made easy profits. In all fairness, he struck me as a man who simply didn't know what he was doing, but was too proud to admit it. Ironically, his tactics would have worked if he had enough money to see it through. Obviously he didn't have enough, and instead, he ruined himself and nearly ruined me in the process."

Vincent shook his head. "Do you really think I would believe you over my brother? I know his faults, and he has never denied them, nor his mistakes. So why would he lie in this instance? He claimed that you, and you specifically, caused him to fail."

"I can't imagine why he singled me out for blame, and I suppose I will never know, since he's deceased. But I'm obviously wasting my breath professing my innocence to you, when you refuse to see beyond the few facts you have been told. So be it. But if you believe all that, why would you help my family?"

"What makes you think I've helped them?"

George stiffened. It was the tone that alarmed him. "What have you done?"

Vincent didn't answer. The moment was at hand, the moment he had worked for, when all he had to say was, "Paid you back in kind," and he couldn't say it. He couldn't go on with this. Not because he believed Ascot; he didn't. But he was himself as much to blame for Albert's death as Ascot was. He hadn't pulled the cords that led to Albert's decision, as Ascot had, but he had done nothing to influence that decision either.

He hadn't recognized it before, had merely seen this revenge thing as doing his duty, more or less. But there was guilt involved, his own, for failing to pay more attention to his brother, for failing to develop a relationship with him in which Albert wouldn't have hesitated to bring even this worst failure of his to Vincent's attention, rather than give up all hope and kill himself instead.

Their parents had spoiled and coddled Albert so much that he was unable to stand on his own after their deaths. He had needed constant bolstering. Having that cut off abruptly by their deaths had hurt him. Vincent could have helped, could have weaned him slowly from his dependence, or at least tried to instill some confidence. Instead he had viewed Albert's weaknesses with disgust, while doing nothing to help his brother overcome them.

"I repeat, what have you done?"

"Nothing that can't be rec—"

"Having somehow managed to buy our home, he then kicked us out of it so we would have no place else to go," Larissa said at the top of the stairs in a dull voice. "Then brought us here so he could seduce me—with no intention of marrying me—which he did quite easily. He took full advantage of my vulnerability in thinking you were dead, Father. He used my grief to aid him, because I needed a distraction from it, and he was that; indeed, he was quite the distraction."

She was staring down at Vincent without expression, as if all emotion had been sucked out of her—or she had no room left for any more. Her brother was standing next to her, staring daggers at Vincent as he slipped his hand into hers to offer comfort. The boy sensed she was in pain even if she wasn't showing it.

Had they heard everything? Yes, they must have for her to have drawn such an accurate conclusion.

But unlike him, they, of course, believed their father without question, that he had done no wrong. And Albert wasn't there to prove otherwise, never would be. Not that it mattered; they would still believe their father, despite the fact that it was Albert who had been ruined, not Ascot.

And if Ascot was telling the truth? No, it wasn't possible, and besides, if Albert had been in the wrong, then Vincent had also been in the wrong to seek revenge on his behalf. That thought didn't sit well with him at all—indeed, positively sickened him—yet it was no worse than what he was feeling now, looking up at Larissa. Such utter dread. He felt as if he had just lost the most valuable thing in his life, and so he had, her respect, her sympathy—her love.

He *should* continue with his revenge for his brother's sake, but he couldn't, because of her. Yet he was going to suffer the consequences either way. Even if he set everything to rights, it would not make a difference with her. He'd sought retribution against a man she saw as innocent, and used her to do it. She'd never forgive him for that. Not even if he managed to convince her that her father was the real culprit. Not that he could, when he only had Albert's letter as proof, and she could claim that was fake.

Yet he had to try. The fear washing over him that he had lost her was more than he could bear.

He said, "There is a letter that will at least explain my actions—"

"I don't doubt you had good reasons for doing what you did," she cut in. "Does that excuse harming the innocent to gain your goal?"

"No," he was forced to reply. "No, the goal became merely an excuse, once I met you."

She blushed. He knew she understood he was saying her seduction had been personal, had nothing really to do with the revenge. But as he'd known, it made no difference. Nor was he allowed to explain further. Her father had recovered by then from his shock in hearing that his daughter had been compromised. He was quite straightforward in his reaction. No demand for marriage, just a very furious fist that caught Vincent by surprise. The Ascots were gone by the time he regained his senses.

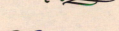

Chapter 21

"She didn't take her Christmas ornaments with her when she left? I wonder why, when they hold such great sentimental value for her."

Vincent didn't answer Jonathan Hale or acknowledge his presence. He didn't want the company, but hadn't thought to tell his butler that he wasn't receiving visitors today. He'd been sitting there in his parlor, alone, staring at Larissa's Christmas tree and recalling that day it was decorated, the enjoyment he'd had, the laughter . . .

He'd felt a part of something that day, rather than the outsider always looking in, as was usually the case for him. That was Larissa's doing. She shared with everyone, excluded no one. She'd made even his servants feel that her tree was their tree, got Jonathan involved in its decoration just because he happened to be there. For her it was an event that began the sharing of the season.

He didn't answer Jonathan, because he was afraid he wouldn't be able to get any words out without their sounding as choked as he felt. But the viscount either didn't notice his preoccupation or chose to overlook it.

Jonathan knew Larissa was gone, that her father had taken her away, and that their whereabouts were presently unknown. He wasn't happy about that, and Vincent was surprised he hadn't asked, "Have you found her yet?" which was his usual first inquiry when he stopped by each day now, and had been for the last week. The painting, his reason for coming there, was rarely mentioned anymore. It had become quite secondary in importance to his pursuit of Larissa.

"Some of them had been made by her mother, you know," Jonathan continued. "A few were even made by her grandparents, and one, that she prized the most, a great-grandfather had whittled. Seems to be somewhat of a tradition in her family, the making of Christmas ornaments. Found that rather quaint myself. Even contemplated making an ornament and giving it to her as a Christmas present, but gave up that idea quick enough. Just ain't talented in that way."

Vincent sighed and finally glanced at his visitor. "There is no news to report," he said, hoping that would send Jonathan on his way.

"Didn't think there would be. I'm just in the habit of coming by daily now. Didn't think you'd mind, and I've decided to take it upon myself to cheer you up."

"I don't need cheering."

"Course you don't," Jonathan said dryly. "You aren't the least bit sick to your guts with missing her. It's too bad you didn't realize sooner that you'd been lying to yourself all along about her."

"Wouldn't have taken you for a man to jump to false conclusions, Jon."

Jonathan chuckled. "Still lying to yourself, or just to me?"

"Go home," Vincent mumbled.

"And let you wallow in all this misery by yourself?" Jonathan said as he dropped down on the sofa beside Vincent. "Now, here I thought the old adage was that misery loves company. I know I ain't enjoying wallowing in mine alone."

"You know bloody well that Larissa would only have been another acquisition for you. You didn't form any deep attachment to her."

"True, which is why my misery is quite mild compared to yours."

"I'm *not* miserable."

Jonathan snorted over that denial. "You're so deep in the doldrums you can no longer see daylight. 'Fess up, man, you were an utter fool not to get the gel engaged to you while you had the chance."

"You don't understand what was going on here," Vincent gritted out.

Jonathan raised a brow. "Apparently not," he allowed, but added, "Did you?"

"Excuse me?"

"Did you realize that she was in love with you? I saw it, though I tried my damnedest to ignore it, of course. Didn't fit with my plans, after all, for her to get so attached elsewhere that my millions wouldn't tempt her. True love just don't come with a price tag, unfortunately."

"I really don't want to talk about this."

"Why not? Or don't you plan to do things right, if given a second chance?"

A second chance? Vincent hadn't thought that far ahead. He *was* making an effort to find Larissa. He *did* plan to lay the truth at her feet, all of it. But he wasn't very hopeful that it would do any good, other than to clear his conscience. And after nearly a week had gone by, he wasn't very hopeful that he'd ever see her again.

He didn't expect her to personally come back to collect what she'd left behind, but he had counted on at least someone, even if only a servant, showing up to do so. But she hadn't sent anyone by to claim her jewels from him. She still didn't even know where those furnishings of hers had been stored. Demanding one or the other would have given him someone to have followed to lead to her, but no one had come.

Hotels and inns had been searched. He had people scouring the whole town and watching Ascot's office around the clock. The ship George had returned in was still in the harbor waiting for permission to dock, so at least he was still in the country. But there was simply no clue as to where he had taken his family off to.

Jonathan apparently got tired of waiting for an answer to his last question. With a sigh he said, "I have a confession to make."

Vincent winced mentally. "Don't. I'm not in the mood for confessions."

"Too bad," Jonathan grumbled. "Because this one is coming whether you listen or not. I came to you to find *La Nymph* for me, not just because I desire to own that painting. There are countless others I could have hired to find the painting, and for much less cost to me. I came to you in particular because I like you, Vincent, I like your style, like the fact that you've never tried to ingratiate yourself with me to get something out of me, as is the case with most people I know. I have no friends, you know, no real friends, that is."

"Nonsense, you don't go anywhere that people don't flock to your side—"

"Leeches, the lot of them," Jonathan cut in, disgust in his tone. "They don't care about me or what I'm feeling, they only care about how they can manage to get some of my money into their pockets. And that's always been the case, even when I was a child. I was born rich, after all."

"Why are you telling me this?" Vincent asked uncomfortably.

Jonathan's cheeks bloomed with a bit of color, but he still admitted, "Because I had great hopes that you would become the close friend I've never had. And since nothing else has worked to accomplish that thus far, I'm falling back on the old premise that confidences are a sound basis for developing lasting friendships. And besides, you don't seem to have any close friends yourself. Do you?"

Vincent saw no reason to deny it. "No."

"Well then—"

"You haven't gathered yet that I am rather reclusive?" Vincent pointed out.

"Course I have, which is one of the things I like about you. And just because I flit about here and there doesn't mean I enjoy doing so, just that I'm so bloody lonely, I crave companionship of any sort, even from sycophants, if that's all that's available."

Vincent was beginning to get embarrassed over these "confidences," not so much because Jonathan felt a sudden need to pour out his guts, but because his confession was sounding much too familiar. He hadn't realized they had quite so much in common, neither of them willing to trust any-one enough to get close to them, neither of them willing to risk being hurt if anyone did.

"Are you feeling sorry for me yet?" Jonathan asked hopefully.

"No."

"Bloody hell . . ."

"But you're welcome to stay for dinner."

The viscount laughed.

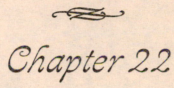

Chapter 22

*I*ronically, Larissa was sitting in front of a Christmas tree at the same time that Vincent was. She was also alone, also recalling the decoration of that other tree. This one wasn't hers and hadn't been preserved well, was mostly brown now, with pitifully broken branches and a pile of fallen needles beneath it that the servants couldn't manage to keep up with. It belonged to the Applebees, good friends of her father's who still lived in Portsmouth. He had taken her and Thomas straightaway there after they'd left Vincent's town house.

Despite Larissa's state of shock when they arrived there, it wasn't lost on her that she hadn't once considered the Applebees as an option when she had agonized over where to take her brother when they lost their home. She would have thought of them eventually, because they really were very old friends of her father's, and she *had* thought of them after she was already moved into Vincent's house, as well as her many childhood friends in Portsmouth, any one of whom would have opened his or her door to her. But by then she had conveniently ignored their existence for the simple fact that she had *wanted* to stay in the baron's home.

Of course, Thomas's illness had been the deciding factor; at least she had convinced herself of that at the time. It was better for him not to make that long trip to Portsmouth while he still had that lingering fever. But they could have managed it, could have sealed up a coach against drafts and got him there as quickly as possible if it had been necessary. Vincent's offered hospitality had made it unnecessary. And Larissa's desire to get to know Vincent better had kept her from considering those other options, even if she hadn't owned up to that at the time.

They had been staying with the Applebees now for nearly a week. It had taken that long for the shock to wear off completely for Larissa. The knowledge that she had been used in a plot for revenge had utterly crushed her. Everything she had supposed about Vincent Everett had been wrong. She had fallen in love with someone who wasn't real, who was a complete fake.

Her father had wanted to comfort her, but after her first outburst of tears when he tried, he had decided the best way to help her get over her heartache was to not discuss it at all, which meant not discussing Vincent. She was grateful for that. She really couldn't bear to talk about him yet, when just thinking about him could start the tears flooding again. But she had been in such a state of despair that she hadn't done much communicating with her father at all yet.

She still didn't even know what had kept him from returning to London for so long. If he had mentioned it, and she supposed he probably had, she hadn't been listening. When she was around, a lot of whispering tended to go on. The Applebees were kind, but if they had been told why she was mired in such misery, they no doubt pitied her.

They were a large family. William and Ethel's four children had married and had young families of their own, and all came to visit their parents at this special time of the year. The house was full. It was a large house, though, so there had been plenty of room for the Ascots, and Thomas had many youngsters to keep him quite occupied. A blessing that, because if her father might be kindly avoiding the subject of her unhappiness, her brother certainly wouldn't have if he could have found her alone. Fortunately, with so many people in the house, it was rare to find anyone alone— until today. The Applebees' four married children had all left to go back to their respective homes that morning.

Because of that mass exodus, Larissa had had the parlor to herself for several hours now. No more pitying whispers. No more attempts to cheer her when she couldn't be cheered. But no more relief either, with the numbness of her shock finally fading. And much too much introspection now and mental browbeating—and anger.

The anger had sneaked up on her, not really un-expected, just all at once it was there and a lot of it, and now bitterly contained just below the surface. Having been used and deceived so easily marked her clearly as a naive fool. And Vincent had done it so easily. That was the quelling blow. She'd almost begged him to dupe her. Every tactic he'd used on her had worked, not because he was so adept at fooling people, but because she had wanted to believe that he cared about her.

Good God, he must have hated touching her, hated making love to her, despising her family as he did. And how he must have laughed at how easily she had succumbed to his seduction and his lies. Everything between them had been a lie, everything she had believed about him, a lie . . .

"Do you want to stay here with Thomas while I return to London?"

The question came from her father, who had just entered the room. At least she heard him right off this time. She recalled a number of times in the last week when he'd had to wave his hand in front of her face and repeat himself to try and get her attention.

"When are you leaving?" she asked.

"In the morning."

He was going to find them a new home. She vaguely remembered that being discussed last evening during dinner. If he went alone, he'd stay at the London office. If she went with him, he'd need to get them rooms at a hotel. She saw no reason to incur the extra expense. She hadn't asked him about his finances. It wasn't her place to ask. In the few conversations that she'd managed to hear when she wasn't so deep in self-pity, she gathered that he'd found new markets in the Caribbean and was no longer worried on that front.

"I'll stay here," she replied.

"You're feeling better?"

There was a great deal of concern in his expression. There was also some hesitancy in his tone that wasn't like him. Her state of nearly deaf distraction since his return must have begun to seriously worry him. But she saw no reason to hedge about the subject now.

"Better, no. Fully cognizant again, yes."

He smiled gently. "A little absentmindedness never—"

She cut in, "I might as well not have been here, Father, for all the awareness I've had lately. Do you know, I don't even know what detained you from returning home when you were supposed to. Each time it has occurred to me to ask you, we haven't been in the same room, and then I as quickly forgot about it again. But I'm sure Thomas and everyone else knows by now. I'm sure you've mentioned it to me as well . . ."

"Three times, actually." He chuckled, then surprised her by saying, "Damn me, never thought I'd reach the point where I could laugh about any part of that ill-fated trip."

"Ill-fated?"

"From the moment we entered the warmer waters of the West Indies. The island we came to first wasn't a major one, though we were so happy to see land of any sort, we stopped there anyway. But as soon as we docked, we were met by the local magistrate and a full troop of guards, and charged with attacking one of the local plantation owners. The man was there to support the charge, and quite a gruesome account he gave of it, that his plantation house burned to the ground, including his barns, that our ship just sat offshore and continued to rain fire down upon his property for no apparent reason."

"Someone actually did that to him?"

"As it turns out, no. But at the time, Peter Heston was an old and well-respected member of the community whom not a single person on that island would even think of doubting, while I and my crew had never been there before and could have been pirates for all they knew. We were found guilty before there was a trial. The actual trial was a mockery where Heston repeated his ghastly tale. No other witnesses were necessary for us to be sentenced to prison."

"Prison!" she gasped, incredulous. "You were actually put in prison?"

"Yes," he replied. "And with absolutely no hope of getting out of it, when we knew that the entire island thought us guilty."

He shuddered unconsciously. She couldn't even begin to imagine how horrible that experience must have been for him and his crew. He'd never been in jail before, never suffered any real physical hardship that she was aware of. Nor should he ever have experienced anything like that, when he was a good, honest man who would never do anything that might get him arrested, much less sent to prison.

Which was what she couldn't help but point out. "But you didn't do anything!"

"No, and our ship's guns were quite cold to prove it," he agreed.

She frowned, getting a bit confused now. "Then why were you even arrested, much less put to trial?"

"Because our proof of innocence required immediate clarification, which didn't occur."

"For someone to examine the guns?"

"Yes."

"Why didn't they?"

He chuckled again. She was surprised herself now that he could, especially after he replied, "Probably because we were about to be lynched on the spot. This was midmorning, you see. And quite a few people had noticed the town guard heading for the docks and followed them. There was a huge crowd by the time we docked, and everyone there was able to hear Heston's accusations. Understandably, the magistrate wanted to break that up quickly, and could only do so by getting us off the dock and into his jail."

"When it would only have taken a moment or two for verification?"

"It was a very tense situation, Rissa. There were other plantation owners in that crowd who were no doubt thinking it could have been *their* houses that we might have destroyed. And when an issue becomes personal like that, emotions can be quite heated. We really were in danger of that mob of angry islanders taking the law into their own hands. Frankly, we were rather glad to be put behind bars until the matter could be straightened out. Knowing ourselves innocent, we didn't really doubt at the time that it would be straightened out, so we were more concerned with the angry crowd than with the charges being filed against us."

"Yes, I suppose the immediate threat would have been of more concern," she agreed. "But you said the man's house hadn't really burned down. Why weren't you released after that was discovered."

"No, I said no one else had done it to him," he corrected her.

She blinked. "He burned down his own house?"

George nodded. "But that didn't come to light soon enough to keep us out of prison. And at the time, the magistrate had two completely conflicting accounts on the matter, so whom do you think he would be inclined to believe?"

"Heston, of course."

"Exactly. The man's plantation really had burned to the ground. Our ship's guns hadn't been fired. These were facts that we were assured were both going to be investigated right after we were all secured in the jail. But too much time had passed, on getting us secured and getting the crowd to finally disperse. And since it wasn't immediately proven that the guns weren't heated the least bit from use, it couldn't be proven at all. Yet there was a burned down plantation, proof for the other side, and the word of one of their own well-known and respected citizens."

Larissa shook her head. "How did the truth finally get discovered?"

"When Peter Heston's wife finally returned to the island. She had been there that day when Heston went completely mad. She had known his mind wasn't quite right for a long time, but she had never warned anyone, since his increasingly strange behavior had seemed harmless. But early that morning she came upon him starting the fires. He was raving that there were pirates hiding on the property and the only way to flush them out was to give them no place to hide by burning everything to the ground."

"There weren't any, though?"

"No, it was all in his mind. She tried to stop him, of course. But he didn't recognize her. He thought her one of the pirates and tried to kill her as well."

"How horrible for her."

"Yes, though she did manage to escape, and by the quickest means possible. Unfortunately, that was by boat. They lived on the coast, had their own small dock where Heston kept a fishing vessel. She used that, leaving the island completely rather than going to town to get help."

"I think I would have rather been out in the water where he couldn't reach me than still on the island where he might catch up to me, if I were her."

"Yes, I suppose you're right. Never looked at it from her perspective, merely from my own, which included her long delay in returning. I would have preferred she come straight to town to report what had happened, thus leaving my crew and me out of the incident completely, but she was so frightened by having her own husband not recognize her, call her a pirate and try to kill her, that she wanted only to get as far from him as possible."

"Where did she go?"

"She had a daughter by her first marriage, who lived on a nearby island. Unfortunately the daughter wasn't home, was on a shopping trip to the mainland."

"Unfortunately?"

"It was the daughter who convinced her that she had to return to get help for Heston, who was obviously quite crazy now, before someone did get hurt by him. Heston's wife had been thinking only of her own safety, which included never returning to her own home. Which was why so much time passed before she did return and the truth was learned."

"Why was there no one else around to witness the fire and how it started? Had they no servants at all?"

"That was one of my own questions, answered by one of the jailers. It was common knowledge that Heston had had bad crops for three out of the last four years. Other plantation owners in the area had suffered from the same bad weather, but it wasn't all a weather problem, not for all three of the bad years. Most of it was likely part of his decline; he simply wasn't attending to his crops properly. But the Hestons were barely making a living by then, because of so many failed crops. The plantation workers were seasonal, so none were around this time of the year. But the house servants had been let go a few years ago. And they lived on the far east end of the island, with no other neighbors close by."

"It is amazing indeed that you can laugh about any of that misadventure."

He grinned at her. "It really wasn't that much of a hardship, their prison. What I find amusing myself is there was no one else in it. The place had been closed up for years. They had to open it and clean it up just for our benefit. There was even a debate to just keep us in the jail instead, though it was finally decided the accommodations there just weren't big enough to contain an entire ship's crew."

"The island was that small?"

"Compare it to one of our country villages and you can imagine the size, and how everyone would know everyone else, which tends to keep down crime. The only reason they even had a prison on the island was it had many years ago been converted from an old fort, which was no longer in use. But we were well fed for our brief sojourn, and not mistreated. The worst part of it all was our boredom—they had yet to decide how to put us to work—and our outrage and sense of hopelessness. In fact, we spent all our time there plotting escape, which we probably would have succeeded at eventually had we been forced to stay there much longer."

"What happened to Peter Heston?"

"Considering he went berserk in town when he saw his wife there, and tried once again to kill her, proving to everyone just how crazy he is now, he's been moved to another island that has a religious order which runs a house to care for the aged and mentally imbalanced. He'll live out his days under the supervision of the nuns there."

"And the townspeople who convicted you out of hand, based on one man's word?"

"Oh, they were duly repentant, so much so that we have been given exclusive shipping rights to all their crops for the next five years."

Larissa raised a brow at her father's new grin. "You find that adequate recompense?"

"Hardly." He chuckled. "Particularly after it came to light that the island was dying due to being so far off the normal shipping lines that they couldn't get ships to come their way."

She huffed indignantly. "So you will be a benefit to them if you agree to contract their crops."

"Certainly, but it satisfied my own goals," he replied. "I will in fact probably have to buy another ship or two to accommodate an entire island—now that I know my old markets are available again."

She could have wished that the conversation had not turned indirectly to the Everetts. But the fact was inescapable that had Albert Everett not forced her father to seek new markets in the West Indies because he stole his old ones, he wouldn't have spent time in prison, would never have had to leave England, so they wouldn't have lost their house—and she wouldn't have met Vincent.

"I am glad you can find something amusing about all this," she said bitterly. "I can't. I thought you were dead. I thought nothing else could have kept you away from home for so long. I imagined shipwrecks, horrible storms, yes, even pirates. Never would I have imagined you detained in a prison, because I know you would never do anything that might break any laws."

He put his arms around her, advising, "Let it go,

Rissa. It's all over now. I'm home, safe, in good health, and have even benefited from the mishaps of the journey. Don't be angry on my account."

"I'm not, I'm furious that the Everetts have done us such an injustice and yet won't pay for it."

"We know how pointless revenge is."

"I know." She sighed.

"And you don't mean *the* Everetts, you mean Vincent Everett in particular. His brother apparently met justice at his own hand."

Chapter 23

$\mathcal{A}$lbert wasn't dead.

It took a while for Vincent to assimilate that fact. He thought hoax. He thought cruel joke. He even thought of George Ascot. After all, how better for Ascot to completely absolve himself of any wrongdoing than by imparting the information contained in the letter that was delivered to Vincent, which painted Ascot as innocent? And it was hand-delivered by a sailor. There was no proof that Albert had written the letter; even his signature could have been a copy.

That thought didn't last long. The letter was

from Albert. The tone in it was his, impossible to duplicate without knowing him well. And references were made that Ascot couldn't have been aware of, without seeing the first letter.

Albert wasn't dead.

It should have been elating news and just that, instead of the incredible shock it was. But then it came with a confession that just about everything in Albert's first letter had been lies and excuses. He placed all blame now where it belonged, on himself. No apologies, not even for giving the wrong impression about his death. Albert hadn't realized he had done so, so he had no idea that Vincent might have picked up the gauntlet for him.

I know you were probably expecting to never hear from me again. I was rather foxed when I wrote you that farewell letter, but I do vaguely recall saying I would never be back. That hasn't changed. I have no desire to ever return to England, where I feel so inadequate to my peers. Where I live now, everything is on an equal footing. Even a beggar can pick himself up by his bootstraps and start over. Which is what I've done.

I did think you might like to hear of my progress, in getting my life in order. And perhaps a better explanation is due, at least a sober one this time, of what brought me to complete failure.

It was so hard to compete with you, brother. You were such a bloody success. Everything you touched turned to gold. I know I shouldn't have felt a need to compete with that, but I did, and that was where I went wrong. Success didn't come to me quick enough, so I tried to rush it. And when that didn't work, I turned more and more to drink, which was truly my downfall.

It got to where I didn't know what I was doing half the time. I hired captains who were less than honest. One was rumored to have been a pirate in his younger years, but since he promised to make me rich, I ignored the rumors. I let them advise me. Everything they told me sounded reasonable; at least when I was foxed it did. But they were under the mistaken impression, which I gave them, of course, that I had an endless supply of blunt backing me. Well you might imagine how some business strategies might work in that case, where they wouldn't otherwise.

271

I'm not making excuses. I've done that all my life, but no more. My failure was the culmination of a lot of bad decisions, all of them mine. I never should have started something that I had no experience in, and when it began to turn sour, I wallowed in self-pity and drink instead of seeking proper help. I was blaming everyone else at the time, including other shippers, because I simply couldn't own up to the fact that I didn't know what I was doing. So someone else had to be the culprit, not I. Childish, I know, but at least I can recognize that now.

I left England in a panic, of course. My letter to you then might have indicated that, though I confess I don't recall everything I said to you in it. Ironic that neither of my two ships was in port at this moment of desertion, so I stowed away on another ship—and was discovered the first day out to sea and put to work scrubbing decks. At least they didn't boot me off the ship in the middle of the ocean.

I haven't had a drink since I left England, nor do I want one. Being completely broke on my arrival in America, I had the choice of begging or getting a job. Pride notwithstanding—that had been completely crushed when I was on my knees swabbing decks—I found a job as a baker's helper. Really nice chap, the baker. He's taken me under his wing, teaching me his craft, and is even talking about expanding, now that I've become so adept with the ovens. I don't mind saying my muffins are good enough to drool over.

I don't expect to become rich here. I no longer have a burning desire to do so. I find satisfaction now in a simple day's work and wage. Even my pride has returned, due to the praise of our customers.

I hope this letter reaches you before Christmas, and leaves you with a smile and the assurance that you no longer need to worry on my account. My gift to you is that baby brother has finally grown up. Do keep in touch, Vince. The only thing that I miss about England is you.

The letter was a nice gift, would have been even nicer if it had arrived before Christmas as intended, before Vincent confronted George Ascot with what he had thought to be the truth. He wasn't going to make excuses for himself either.

He'd been wrong in his beliefs, and wrong to seek revenge of any sort, particularly when, as Ascot had said, a little investigation would have pointed out some of the discrepancies in his brother's false accusations.

Once more he was mired in guilt, and not just for failing his brother. Albert had managed to land on his feet and was getting on admirably with his life, while Vincent now had to deal with his own shortcomings. He had wronged an innocent family, severely wronged them, and he wasn't sure how to make amends for that, if he even could. Returning what he had taken from them wouldn't be enough, not to satisfy him. Nothing was going to help there, when in his rash undertaking he had ended up hurting the woman he had come to love.

Chapter 24

$\mathcal{G}$eorge Ascot was finally found. Two days before the New Year arrived, he showed up at his company office in London. He even spent the night there, giving Vincent ample time to arrange around the clock surveillance so that he could be followed when he left. It also gave him the opportunity to speak privately with Ascot himself.

Apologies were owed, whether they would be accepted or not. He at least wanted to assure the man that the vendetta was over. He didn't expect the visit to assuage his guilt. Not even complete forgiveness or understanding would do that, when he couldn't manage to forgive himself.

The office was locked when he arrived. He chose the earliest hour possible just after dawn, well before Ascot's clerk was due. He was aware he might catch Ascot still sleeping, but they would at least be assured of privacy at that hour.

George hadn't been sleeping. But he certainly wasn't receptive to his visitor either. Having opened the door, he took one look at Vincent and began to close it again.

"A moment is all I ask," Vincent said.

"When it's all I can do to keep from bloodying your face, a moment is too long."

George's expression said he wasn't exaggerating. He looked absolutely furious. And he was a big man. He might well be able to do considerable "bloodying" even if Vincent defended himself. Of course, Vincent's guilt wouldn't let him defend himself, but neither would a beating help him to get rid of it, so he would prefer discourse to violence.

"I am here to offer apologies and an explanation, though the latter is more for my benefit than yours."

"An apology when you think me guilty? Or have you found out that I'm not the villain you took me for?"

"I set out to ruin you. An eye for a eye. I make no excuses for that, other than I really did think you indirectly responsible in contributing to my brother's death. But you were correct that I was lax in not verifying the facts. I have since learned the truth."

"Not from me, you didn't," George said bitterly. "You refused to believe me."

"Would you have taken the word of a stranger over that of your brother?"

"If I had such a weak-kneed brother, I just might," George said.

It was the contempt in the tone, rather than the actual words, that caused Vincent to flush with embarrassment. "He was weak, yes, but he wasn't known to lie. However, he was also foxed when he wrote his parting letter, doesn't even recall much of what he said in it, and to give him his due, he didn't suspect that I might mistake his intentions and seek revenge on his behalf."

"Doesn't recall? Are you saying he didn't kill himself after all?"

"I have only just received another letter from

him, a sober one this time. He has settled in America. He now takes all blame onto himself for his failure here."

"Which leaves you having pursued vengeance against an innocent party."

"Given the information I had, in my mind, it wasn't fair that you would escape without any consequences at all, when you had set out to ruin a competitor and had succeeded, perhaps more than you had planned, but succeeded nonetheless. But my original information was wrong, so yes, I have myself become the villain in this whole debacle, due to my mistaken beliefs. For this I do humbly apologize and will make amends as you see fit. I begin with these."

"What is this?" George asked skeptically, accepting the packet of documents.

"The deed to your home, in your name, all debt satisfied. The address is also there, where your furnishings are stored. I have also set about correcting the rumors about your financial straits. Your presence again in England confirms the falseness of the original rumors. If you have any further difficulty over this matter—"

"I will see to it myself."

"As you wish," Vincent replied, realizing he was insulting the man in implying that he couldn't handle the situation on his own. "I merely didn't want you to have to be bothered correcting what I set in motion, if I have overlooked any other effects it might have had."

"If you wish to make amends, do so by staying away from me and my family, so we can forget that you exist. What you did to me is moot, even somewhat understandable. What you did to my daughter—"

"Had nothing to do with this."

"Do you really expect me to believe that?"

"It's true only that had I not begun this, I wouldn't have met Larissa. But from the moment I saw her, I was smitten beyond anything in my experience. I'll admit I lied to myself. She was off-limits to me by normal means. I couldn't marry her because she was your daughter, the daughter of an enemy. Yet I couldn't not try to make her mine. So revenge became merely an excuse for me to ignore my own conscience in the matter."

"You're talking about an innocent child that you took advantage of!"

"I'm talking about the *woman* I love. She's a child only in your mind, sir. And had you not returned when you did, I would have tossed all my efforts to the wind to obtain the only goal that has any meaning for me now—I would have begged her to marry me."

George snorted his skepticism. "Convenient to say when you know she won't have you, that she despises you for what you did to her."

Vincent sighed. "Not convenient, merely late in the discovery. Even on Christmas eve, I hadn't yet realized just how much I love her. I had done everything possible to keep her in my house. I lied to her, misled her, just to keep her from leaving me."

"You *admit* that?"

"Yes. I was still convinced that marriage was out of the question, a betrayal, as it were, to my brother. But on Christmas morning she finally demanded to know if my intentions were honorable as she'd assumed or not, and if not, she was leaving me. I knew then that revenge was meaningless in comparison to losing her. But before I could let her know that, you arrived."

"You hardly sounded as if you had just come to that realization during our discourse."

"My anger with you got in the way."

"I will consider that fortunate for my family," George replied stiffly. "Now if you are finished, Lord Everett, I don't believe we have anything further to say."

"Will you allow me to see your daughter? She is owed an apology as well—"

"She is owed some peace over this matter, or don't you realize how devastated she was by your revelations. She is only just beginning to recover. Stay away from her."

Chapter 25

Stay away from her? Vincent couldn't. He would have liked to have permission to approach Larissa, but with it or without it, he had to see her. But she didn't return to London so that he could.

George moved back into the London house, had their furnishings fetched and reinstalled, and filled the place with servants again. He'd been quite busy, taking care of normal business that required his attention after such a long absence, as well as visiting all those merchants who had panicked at the first hint that he had deserted England.

The reports that Vincent was receiving were

that a lot of groveling was done by the merchants. Not unexpected of a merchant class that depended on the goodwill of their customers. Whether George was forgiving or not was moot and of little interest to Vincent. The people he had following George were reporting basic actions, they weren't getting close enough to overhear conversations.

The empty town house was a home again by the end of the year, but a home without children; at least Larissa and Thomas hadn't returned to it yet. Vincent was beginning to worry that Larissa wasn't going to return at all, and because of him. Not an unfounded worry. George could have sent her word about their meeting and his desire to see her. Her absence in London could well be her response to that. Which was why, when Ascot left London, Vincent was not far behind him.

Portsmouth turned out to be the final destination. Vincent wasn't surprised. He'd actually had the inns and hotels searched there, being aware that was where the Ascots had lived prior to relocating in London. With no luck, of course. But a little information had been gathered about the Applebees before he knocked on their door the next day, so he knew these were old friends of the Ascots.

He wasn't denied entry. He might have been. But the Applebees' butler apparently hadn't been warned to turn him away. But then the Ascots probably hadn't expected him to show up in Portsmouth either. He still didn't hold much hope of actually seeing Larissa, though. She'd be told he was there. It would be her decision and likely a denial. But he got lucky . . .

Larissa stopped halfway down the stairs when she saw Vincent being led to the parlor. The urge was to turn about abruptly. She didn't want to talk to him again—ever. But it would be cowardly to rush back to her room, and besides, her anger wouldn't let her do it. She wasn't numbed by shock this time. Her anger brought her down to the bottom of the stairs, where he had moved to the moment he saw her.

She was going to slap him, as hard as she could. An action worth a thousand words so there would be no mistaking what she felt for him now. But she didn't do it. Standing that close, she was caught by the golden glow in his eyes, then entrapped for several long moments as her body reacted in myriad ways to being near to him again.

Good God, how could she still be attracted to

him? How could she desire him still, when she despised him beyond reason? When his hand reached toward her cheek, her knees nearly buckled. His caress was imminent. It was going to destroy her resolve and make her forget, briefly, why she never wanted to see him again.

"Larissa—"

"Don't touch me!"

She jumped back, nearly tripped on the stairs. Her pulse was racing. That had been too close, her senses returning nearly too late to stop him.

"Don't touch me again," she repeated in a calmer, though scathing tone. "You use that as a tactic to bend my will to yours, but I'm aware of that now and won't be—"

"Larissa, marry me."

Moisture sprang immediately to her eyes. "You ask too late."

"I know, but to not ask would be one more regret to add to the rest."

She should have turned to leave then. She should have ignored the pain in his eyes that was ripping at her heart. That she couldn't bear to walk away from him yet infuriated her, and that came out in her tone.

"Nothing you can say will rectify what you've done, so why do you put us both through this?"

"Because I need to wipe the slate clean, and there are still things you don't know that must be confessed before I can do that."

"Your *needs* are no longer a concern of mine."

"Hear me out at least. It won't take much of your time. And I actually have more fuel for you to add to the fire, lies I told you, and why I did."

"I've already realized that just about everything you've ever said to me was a lie," she replied. "There's no need to confirm that."

"Hardly everything," he said with a sigh.

She had the feeling he wanted to caress her again. Was he experiencing the same pull that she was, which was almost irresistible? Very well, so perhaps he hadn't hated touching her, hadn't laughed at how easy it had been to seduce her. Perhaps this powerful attraction really was mutual. But that changed nothing. He had still used her to get at her father. He hadn't hesitated to trample the innocent on the path to his goals.

It was probably guilt that had brought him there. She understood why he might be feeling it now. But she didn't care. She was done feeling sympathy for a man who didn't deserve it. And assuaging his guilt would only be a benefit to him. It would be nothing but pain to her, to hear it all spelled out, how he'd used her.

Yet the words came out before she could stop them. "Make your confession, but please keep it brief."

He nodded. He smiled softly. He had to stuff his hands in his pockets to keep from touching her.

"The lie began from the start. I brought you to my house because from the moment I first saw you, I wanted you. That had nothing at all to do with your father. He would have been easy enough to find at his office, once he returned. Fortunately, you didn't point that out when I mentioned needing an address so I could find him."

"I was too upset that night to think of anything," she said in her defense.

"That was rather obvious and to my benefit, because I was so taken with you, I wasn't thinking very clearly myself, so probably wouldn't have been able to come up with a better excuse to move you into my house. But it worked. You moved in. And then I faced the dilemma of how to keep you under my roof as long as possible, because I couldn't bear the thought of being denied even one extra day with you, when I'd already accepted the fact that our time together would be limited, and end, once your father returned. Keeping you without funds or the need for them was my solution to that."

"Need for them?"

"You had mentioned your brother would need a physician, so I had mine summoned for you. His visit wasn't an annual occurrence as you were told, he was there specifically to see to your brother."

"One kindness on your part doesn't excuse—"

"Rissa, that was no kindness, that was to keep you from selling any of your possessions to pay for a physician, which would leave you with coins in hand to find lodging elsewhere. To further insure that you wouldn't be selling anything, I invented that excuse to lock up your jewels. My servants are actually all quite trustworthy."

"Had I requested them back?"

"The key to my safe would have conveniently— for me—gone missing."

After that confession, it occurred to her to ask, "There was never a theft at the warehouse where our things were stored, was there?"

"No. I merely had anything of value there

moved to a different location, in case you wanted
to go there to see what was left. It would have all
been returned to you, which was why I mentioned
my own involvement in searching for the 'thieves,'
so you wouldn't wonder at how easily the items
could be recovered. Stealing from your family
wasn't on my agenda."

"No, just thoroughly ruining us."

The bitterness in her tone was thick enough to
cut, bringing a frown to his brow. "Are you deliberately failing to see that these are two unrelated
issues?"

"Hardly unrelated when you managed to accomplish two goals with one—"

"From the moment you entered my house," he
cut in, "your father was all but forgotten in my
mind. I lived and breathed *you*. You consumed my
every thought. Everything I did was done to obtain
you. But I convinced myself that the only way I
could have you was with the excuse of revenge. I
couldn't have you by normal means, couldn't
marry you because your father was my enemy—"

"He was never your enemy."

"At the time he was. In my mind he was. At least
allow that what one believes is a truth for *him* for

however long he believes it. I saw your father as being directly responsible for my brother's ruination, which also made him indirectly responsible for his death. Yet I was merely going to ruin him financially. I wasn't going to exact any harsher revenge. An eye for an eye, as it were. He could rebuild, reestablish. Albert was dead, or so I thought. Your father wasn't."

"Why are you telling me this when it doesn't pertain to me? You seduced me with no intention of marrying me. *That* pertains to me! Admit it."

"I have admitted it. I merely wanted you to know why I felt that I couldn't marry you, and why it finally didn't matter."

"I know why it doesn't matter. My father told me your brother isn't dead as you'd thought. He was your motive; now you have none. That doesn't excuse what passed before."

"He told you that, but he didn't tell you I'd already realized it was over before then, before your father arrived Christmas morning. Or don't you remember what we were discussing just prior to his showing up?"

"I recall you saying you couldn't marry me because of my father."

"After that, Rissa. I realized during that conversation that you were all that mattered to me. I told you so, if you'll try to remember. The vendetta was over as far as I was concerned. I even tried to tell your father that nothing had been done that couldn't be rectified, but you interrupted with your interpretation of what I'd done."

When he was admitting to all these lies, what he was telling her now was to be believed? She'd be a fool to let him dupe her again, but then she was a fool for standing there listening to him at all.

"Are you done confessing?"

It was probably her stiffness that made him realize he was getting nowhere with her, that nothing would breach the shell of her bitterness. His expression turned so sad it nearly made her cry. But she wasn't going to relent, she wasn't . . .

"No, actually, you might as well know that I was in your room that night, the night you thought I was, awake, and driving myself crazy with wanting you. That silly story about sleepwalking was a lie. The locks were put on your doors because I couldn't trust myself not to enter your room again without permission."

"And what you told me of your past, to gain my sympathy?" she recalled. "All lies as well."

"Your sympathy is a wonderful thing, Rissa, and yes, I used it. But it wasn't necessary to invent a pitiful past to stir your compassion. Everything I told you of my childhood was true. I had merely never told anyone else about it before, because I despise pity." He smiled wryly. "Your pity I wanted, though. Your pity is such an amazing thing."

"Your lies were pointless."

"Excuse me?"

"I could have left at any time if I had really wanted to. Your lies wouldn't have stopped me."

"You had your brother to think of, not just yourself. You wouldn't have left without funds."

"No, certainly, but there were a few more valuables stored at my father's office that I never mentioned to you, a titled painting and several antique maps my father had intended to sell, but didn't get around to doing before he left. The maps would have fetched a nice price."

"And the painting is *La Nymph*."

She blinked. "How did you know that?"

His laugh was quite hollow. "A logical guess,

since I happen to have been searching for that painting for a client for several months now, and it was known to be in the possession of a ship owner, just not which one."

"Why that painting in particular?"

"Have you seen it?"

She frowned. "Actually, I recall my father rushing me out of the storeroom the last time I visited the office when he was there, because he didn't want me to see it. He mentioned something about it being inappropriate for innocent eyes, so I assumed it was a nude."

"Indeed, but a rather risqué one by all accounts," he replied. "And my client will likely pay you a half million pounds for it."

She blinked again. "Is he out of his mind?"

"No, just very eccentric, with more money than he will ever be able to spend."

"You're teasing me. I don't find that very nice under the circumstances, but then why should that surprise me?"

He sighed. "I swear I'm not. You know him well enough. It's Jonathan Hale who wants to get his hands on that painting so much that he's hired me to find it. Now I've found it. It's in your possession.

I'm sure he'll be contacting your father about it just as soon as I tell him."

"Why would you tell him, when it will be a benefit to my father? You did realize that, didn't you?"

"If you would stop being suspicious of my motives long enough to think about what I've told you today, you'd have an answer to that. Have you never done anything that you bitterly regret now?"

"Aside from meeting you?"

He blushed, but continued relentlessly, "Didn't you tell me how you despised your father for moving you to London and regretted how you treated him for it?"

"You compare childish pouting to what you did to me?" she demanded incredulously.

"No, I am merely reminding you that none of us are perfect. We cannot always do as we aspire to; we too often act on emotions that shouldn't be released. I wasn't used to being controlled by emotions, Rissa. Good God, I was even under the foolish belief that I didn't have any, since so many years had passed without anything provoking mine. Then I met you and I suddenly had *too* many emotions stirring all at once."

The golden heat was entering his eyes again. She

began to panic. She'd managed to remain unaffected by his closeness this long, or at least to give that impression, but she didn't think she could withstand again being devoured by those seductive eyes of his.

"You've finished. Please go."

"Rissa, I love you. If you're never going to believe anything I say to you again, at least believe that."

She left instead, ran up the stairs to hide behind a locked door where she could cry in peace. She wished he hadn't come. She wished those last words of his weren't going to haunt her, but she knew they would.

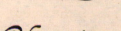

Chapter 26

$\mathcal{L}$arissa didn't go down to dinner that night. Her family was returning to London in the morning, which allowed her to use the excuse of packing to avoid a last night of socializing. A kindness on her part, that she not inflict her rotten mood on the Applebees.

How could she have been so unlucky, to have come downstairs today at the precise moment that Vincent was being led across the hall? And so foolish not to have taken the cowardly route as had been her first impulse, instead of giving him a chance to speak to her.

She could have recovered, eventually, without hearing his grand confession. Now she knew the worst, but also the best—if she could believe it. And there was the rub and the source of her sorrow. She couldn't believe it.

How does one trust again after being so thoroughly lied to? She'd never been lied to before, thus had never figured that out for herself. And Vincent was asking too much of her, to forgive, to forget, to accept him as he was without suspicions. How could she do that when he could lie so convincingly, so expertly, that she'd never be able to know when he was being truthful with her?

Of course, everyone made mistakes and had faults, but not everyone had such ruthless faults as Vincent did. Someone else might be able to overlook them, to say that only love mattered, but she had too many doubts for that someone to be her. Yes, she still loved him. The wrenching in her heart today made that bitterly obvious. But she despised everything he'd done and she'd never get beyond that simple fact long enough to forgive him.

She was dreading going to bed, knowing she wouldn't get much sleep that night. So her father's knock at the door was very welcome, even if the subject that he brought in with him wasn't.

"I was informed that Lord Everett paid you a visit today," he said as he joined her in front of the fireplace where she had been sitting, staring blankly at the dancing flames. "I hadn't realized that he might follow me here to find you, or I would have seen to it that he never get past the door. I hope you know that I had expressly forbidden him to see you, to no avail, obviously."

"It's all right," she replied. "I doubt he'll try to see me again."

"You turned him down, then?"

"You knew he was going to ask?"

"I'd gathered that was his goal, yes. He claims to love you. Do you have reason to doubt that after your experiences with him?"

"Yes—no," she corrected, then with a frustrated sigh, added, "I don't know anymore."

"I'm sorry, Rissa. I know you haven't wanted to talk about what happened. But I have assumed, from your state of melancholy, that you love the man."

"I did. I don't now."

He smiled gently. "Would that it were so easy to

turn love off and on with a few simple words. Here, take these and read them," he said, handing her two letters. "I've had them in my possession for several days now. I wasn't going to show them to you, since they might upset you again, but perhaps that decision was a mistake on my part."

"What are you talking about?"

"Those letters. They were given to me when Everett handed over the deed to our home. I didn't know it until he was gone. How much do you know about the brother?"

"Not much. He rarely spoke of him. When he was mentioned, it was in connection with Vincent's childhood, which was pathetically lonely—he *says* that wasn't one of the many lies he told."

"You don't believe it?"

"I honestly don't know what to believe anymore. As for Albert, they weren't close except for a very brief time when they were young. Albert was their parents' favorite, you see. He went everywhere with them, while Vincent was never included. I gather that Vincent was in the habit of cleaning up his brother's calamities, though, a brotherly duty, as he saw it. Mind you, everything I just told you came directly from Vincent, a known liar."

He ignored the bitter tone, said, "You'll find those letters enlightening, then."

She stared at her father, waited for further explanation. He gave none, merely nodded at the letters now in her hand. She read them, both. They were Albert Everett's letters to Vincent. She had to read the first one again to make sense of it, then once more.

Finally she said, "This first one does paint a rather dastardly picture of you, doesn't it?"

"Yes, from a child crying foul. And Albert even admits it in the second letter, that he hadn't grown up yet, at least not to a point where he would take responsibility for his own actions."

"You would think that Vincent would have suspected as much."

"When, as you say, he didn't really have much association with his brother?"

"You're defending him?" she asked incredulously.

"No, just trying to see this mess from his perspective—and well aware that given the same set of circumstances in my own family, I probably would have acted exactly as he did. Actually, I may well have acted much worse and have called the man out who had so ruined a member of my family that he chose to kill himself."

"But revenge is pointless. You've always said so. You've raised us to believe the same."

"Revenge is, yes, and particularly when you don't have the means to inflict it. But when you have a victim driven to the point of death, and the one responsible escapes without any consequence whatsoever, then it's a matter of trying to visit justice on the guilty one."

"You really *are* defending him."

George chuckled. "No, because we don't really have all the facts and never will have them. Even Albert admits he was drinking heavily most of the time that the events occurred, so wouldn't remember exactly what brought him low. Lord Everett is guilty of drawing his own conclusions. But given the known facts, his conclusions were hard to dispute."

"Not if he had bothered to find out what sort of man you were," she insisted. "And that you would *never* do anything so reprehensible—"

Another chuckle. "You needn't get indignant on

my account at this late stage, Rissa. It's over. Our lot has actually improved because of it. The only casualty involved is you, but even that can be rectified."

"By marrying him?" she snorted.

"Only you can decide your destiny at this point," he replied, and headed toward the door. But he paused there long enough to add, "I read that first letter again and again, and then I played a little 'what if.' I suggest you do the same. Read the first letter and imagine it's from Thomas, grown up to manhood, of course. But imagine that he wrote that to you. Then ask yourself, what would you do about it?"

Chapter 27

$\mathcal{V}$incent wasn't quite certain how it happened, but Jonathan Hale now considered him his best friend. Ironically, Jon wasn't far wrong. Vincent did in fact welcome his company now. He supposed it could just be that he needed the distraction. But Jon was much more relaxed, in thinking them friends, which in turn made him more amusing, so his company really was enjoyed. However, it didn't take much for Vincent to realize that without Jon's visits and amusing chatter, he'd have no break at all from the painful moroseness that otherwise filled his mind from morning till night.

Failure was so alien to him. He succeeded at most all of his endeavors, except the one most important to him, the only one that mattered. And how arrogant, to think he could convince Larissa to give him another chance if he could just talk to her. She did still care for him. He had seen that in her eyes. But it wasn't enough. Would anything be? Laying everything, every lie and little deceit, on the floor before her for a fresh start hadn't helped.

He hoped he had merely tried too soon, that more time was needed for the biting edge of his deception to dull. But if she couldn't find it in her heart to forgive him, or at least to understand why he had done what he had, then no amount of time was going to help.

Jonathan had at least benefited from Vincent's brief visit to Portsmouth. The Ascots hadn't taken advantage of him, knowing how much he would have paid for *La Nymph*. George had charged him only what he felt the value of the painting was, which was much less than what Jon had paid Vincent in commission. Ascot really was as good and honorable as Larissa had made him out to be. Which just made Vincent feel even more rotten.

And how did one get on with one's life, when one refused to cut the cords to do so?

One of the cords Vincent wasn't letting go of was the Christmas tree in his parlor. He wasn't going to remove it. It could rot there, until nothing was left but dead bare branches, but it was staying there in his parlor until Larissa showed up for the ornaments on it.

Jonathan was right, they *were* valuable to her, and Vincent was counting on that, that she wouldn't send just anyone by to fetch them for her, that she would come herself to collect them. And when she did, she wasn't going to be handed a filled trunk that she could immediately leave with, she was going to have to spend a bit of time there removing the ornaments from the tree herself.

It was his last hope. A little time with her alone. And perhaps she might remember, as well, the fun they'd had decorating her tree. He was counting on that, counting on other memories associated with his house to remind her how wonderful their lives could be, if she would give him another chance.

He took precautions as well, going out only when he absolutely had to. She might think she could come there without seeing him, but he had left strict orders that he was to be summoned if she showed up, and not let in at all if he wasn't there, which would force her to return when he was. And so he waited.

She did come, and in the late morning when he was usually home, so she was making no effort to avoid him. He found her still in the hall where she'd been asked to wait. She appeared nervous. It was actually hard to discern, when her beauty overwhelmed him, but he did notice it, the chewing at her lower lip that she stopped when he appeared, her hands clenched tightly in front of her.

It was perhaps that nervousness, rather than her desire to leave soonest, that had her blurting out immediately, "I've come for our Christmas ornaments. I couldn't bring myself to fetch them sooner."

"I understand you'd rather not see me."

"It wasn't that. I just wanted you to have a normal Christmas tree for once. We made do, sharing the Applebees' tree for the remainder of the season. But I knew you wouldn't, that if we stripped your tree, you'd leave it that way."

"Why?"

"Excuse me?"

"Why did it matter to you?" he asked.

"Because it was your first tree."

"So? I've gone this long without having one. I could have gone the rest of my life without having one."

"That's why, because you don't care. Because it saddens me that you don't care."

He smiled gently. "Rissa, a Christmas tree is nothing if you have no one to share it with. You said as much yourself. It symbolizes a season that is celebrated in sharing. Come. Let's share this one for the last time."

He moved to the parlor, didn't wait for her, knew she would follow. He was rather proud of the condition of her tree, watched eagerly as she entered the room and saw it. She was amazed, clearly. He had hoped for a smile, though, instead of just surprise.

"You changed it, brought in a new tree. Why?"

"It's the same tree," he insisted. "I've been pampering it myself, watering it twice a day. It decided to survive a little longer."

He was joking that the tree might have had any say-so in the matter, but she was too sentimental not to agree with him, and with the smile he'd hoped for, she said, "So it did, and quite beautifully, too. I don't believe I've ever stripped a tree looking this healthy before. Are you *sure* you didn't bring in a new one?"

"Did I forget to assure you that I'd never lie to you again?"

She blushed. There it was, standing between them again, everything he'd done, everything he regretted. And how utterly foolish, to let that subject come up so soon. He'd wanted her to relax first, to recall the fun they'd had in this room.

"Do you realize that saying it isn't an assurance, when the assurance could be a lie as well?"

"Your doubt is tangible, Rissa, and understandable. But have you realized that most of the lies were to keep you here? I wanted you so much, I was committed to doing anything in my power to have you come willingly to me. I'm sorry for the deceptions having to do with your father. I made mistakes. I'm far from perfect. But I won't apologize for wanting you, or for making love to you, or for anything I did to make you mine, if only for a little while, because saying I'm sorry for *that* would be a lie."

Though her cheeks were a bit brighter from his bluntness, she didn't reply. She even moved away from him so she could stare at the tree without looking at him. Her expression had given him no clue, either, to how his statements had affected her, other than to embarrass her.

He tried again. "I was never going to marry. But then I was never going to fall in love either. It was an emotion I thought I was immune to. You've proven me wrong. I just wish I had realized it before Christmas day. Had I recognized it sooner, we would have been engaged before your father returned; hell, I might even have dragged you off to Gretna Green to make sure we were married before his return."

He paused, waited hopefully, but she still just stared pensively at the tree. His last chance, and she was shooting it down with her silence. Of course, that was answer in itself. She'd had enough time to harden her resolve. But he hadn't anticipated indifference.

He moved behind her, started to put his hands on her shoulders, but stopped himself, afraid she'd bolt if he touched her. "Rissa, say something."

"I read your brother's letters."

"And?"

"And I might have done the same thing you did."

He went still, held his breath. "You're saying you forgive me?"

"I'm saying I love you and can't find any way around that."

He didn't give her a chance to take it back or try to correct what she'd just said. He swung her around, gathered her close, kissed her deeply. That she yielded immediately was his answer and filled him with such relief, there was barely any room left to contain his joy. She was his again! And he wasn't going to lose her this time.

"You came here with the intention of forgiving me?" he said.

"I thought it might be possible."

Her grin was infectious. He returned it, hugged her tightly. "Elope with me."

"No, we do this the proper way this time. You'll have to speak to my father."

He groaned. "He's made his feelings clear. He doesn't like me."

"You'll find he's probably changed his mind about that," she told him. "He knows I love you. He's the one who made me see that I was being too hard on you. But if I'm wrong, *then* we can elope."

"You really mean that, don't you?" he asked her in amazement.

She cupped his cheeks in her hands so tenderly.

"I was letting my hurt overrule my heart, when I knew deep down that you were still the man I fell in love with. I'm sorry it took so long for my heart to take over again—"

"Shh, it doesn't matter now. Nothing else matters, except that we're together again. I'll speak to your father immediately."

"You'll help me take down the Christmas tree first," she said.

He chuckled. "I knew that tree was going to bring us together again."

"It's almost a shame to take it down, when it's still so green."

"Then don't," he suggested. "Or is that part of the ritual?"

"Well, it does sort of put Christmas to rest until the next year."

"Who says it has to be put to rest? I rather liked your concept of 'sharing.'"

She smiled, reached for his hand to hold it. "We won't need a tree for that."

He brought her hand to his lips. "No, I don't suppose we will."

Chapter 28

"*O*h . . . oh, my."

That didn't quite express Larissa's degree of surprise, it was more indicative of her speechlessness when she finally noticed the large painting hanging on the wall at the head of Vincent's bed.

They had been married that morning, just a small gathering of family and friends. Viscount Hale had wanted to throw them the biggest party London had ever seen, but Vincent had adamantly refused, mentioning something about theaters and what had happened the last time the *ton* got a look at Larissa, and that he'd like to keep her to himself for a while more as they settled into marriage.

Jonathan understood perfectly, if Larissa didn't. She had enjoyed the theater, but she wasn't sure she would enjoy a huge London bash, so she was rather glad her husband had declined the offer.

Her father had welcomed Vincent to the family with open arms, as she had predicted. Her brother hadn't. Having witnessed the turmoil of her emotions while she was falling in love, and blaming many of those tears on Vincent, Thomas had taken a "wait and see" attitude. For him, Vincent was going to have to prove that he could make Larissa happy. She was sure it wouldn't take long, though, when she was already happier than she could ever have thought possible.

"Oh, my," she said yet again, causing Vincent to chuckle this time as he came to stand behind her next to the bed.

She was staring at an exquisitely beautiful, naked young maiden cavorting with four satyrs in a woodland glade. That was the modest description of *La Nymph*. The depicted scene was actually much more lurid, and anyone with any degree of imagination could make whatever he or she wanted to out of it.

"Our wedding gift from Jonathan," Vincent explained, his hands resting on her shoulders.

"We don't have to keep it, do we?"

He laughed. "No indeed, and in fact, it's only on loan to us. He expects it back, though I don't doubt he's glad to be rid of it for a while. He was somewhat amazed to find the notorious effect of the painting quite true, at least for him." He explained to her, briefly, the history of *La Nymph*, ending with, "The day he brought it home, after purchasing it from your father, he ended up visiting four of his mistresses, quite an exhausting experience, I would imagine."

She turned around, stared at him wide-eyed. "He had that many—lady friends?"

His hands began to caress her neck. "More than that, but he only managed to get around to that many that day."

She huffed a bit indignantly. "And there I thought he was interested in me for marriage; at least that is the impression he gave."

"Oh, he was." He grinned. "He did indeed want to marry you."

"When he kept company with so many other women?" she all but snorted.

"What he would have offered you in a marriage was more money than you could ever imagine. He wasn't offering faithfulness. He would have been up front about it, though, explaining to you that variety is the spice of his life. It would have been entirely up to you if you wanted that sort of marriage."

"He actually thought I could be . . . ? Well, *bought* is the word that comes to mind."

Vincent smiled, his thumbs beginning to circle her cheeks, then her earlobes. "He had hoped so. You became his newest goal for a while. But he began to see where your true interest was—and mine as well—and bowed out of the running with no hard feelings. Actually, now that he considers me his best friend, he's quite delighted that you've married me instead."

"A friend, yet he can give you something like that?" she said, nodding at the painting again.

"A joke, sweetheart, in poor taste in that it has nothing to do with love, everything to do with sex, but he meant no harm by it. But then it doesn't have quite the same effect on me as it does on him."

"No?"

"Some people are stimulated by what they see, as in the case of the painting. For others, visual makes no difference; touch is their only stimulation; it must be what they can feel. And for still others, there is emotional stimulation; the heart must be involved."

"You fall into the third category?"

"I'm not sure which might have been the case before I met you, but I'm quite sure which is the case now. Love makes the difference for me. You are my only stimulation."

She hadn't been immune to the caresses she had been receiving, but his words thrilled her beyond measure. "I believe we just might have all three categories covered tonight," she said breathlessly. "Though the latter two are preferred."

"I'll get rid of the first," he offered.

He went to the head of the bed to flip the painting around to the wall. Neither of them was expecting there to be another painting on the back of it, of the exact same scene, just rendered from behind.

They both laughed. "Now, that is too funny," Larissa allowed. "Even the artist realized that not everyone would appreciate his work. Quite determined, wasn't he, that it not be hidden from view?"

Vincent grinned, grabbed a sheet from the bed, and draped it over the painting. "And I'm quite determined that your wedding night be perfect in every way."

He came back to stand before her, cupped her cheeks in his hands. The golden glow was in his eyes, though his expression was intensely serious for a moment.

"I love you so much, I'm not sure how to express it, Rissa. You've brought light into what was darkness. I existed, but I wasn't living. Can you understand what I mean? You filled a void in my life I didn't know I had."

"Don't make me cry," she said, moisture gathering in her turquoise eyes.

He smiled gently just before he hugged her close. "I don't mind your sympathy tears. They show me how much you love me."

"I'd rather show you in other ways."

"You do. You show me in so many ways, but I'll never get enough. I'm so *glad* that you're my wife, Rissa. And I promise to make you glad of it also, every day, for the rest of your life."

She wiped the tears from her eyes, gave him a brilliant smile. "You've already begun."

ALSO BY JOHANNA LINDSEY...

Heart of a Warrior

Available in hardcover

In the world of romantic fiction, no one compares to Johanna Lindsey. A magnificent storyteller, Lindsey weaves together endearing characters, enthralling adventure, and pulsating passion to create moving stories that touch the heart. Now Lindsey returns with a magical tale of star-crossed love and two powerful people drawn together by irresistible desire.

She is proud and strong, a woman who vows that no man will plumb the depths of her soul. He is a warrior, powerful and brave, a man who fearlessly fights for what he wants. And he wants her...

*B*rittany Callaghan stared in the mirror above her dresser, satisfied with the results. The blouse was sequined, fancy, but not too sexy. The jewelry was demure, nothing flashy. The long velvet skirt was elegant, slim, slit to the knee. It had taken her two hours to get ready, not that she needed that much time to look nice, but tonight was special, so she'd devoted more time than usual in her preparations.

Her makeup, applied just right, brought out the deep green of her eyes. Her roommate Jan had done her hair, managing to get the long mass of copper into a tight coiffure that would have earned Jan praise in her beauticians class. They made a great pair as roommates, swapping each others skills as needed. Brittany could fix just about anything that went wrong in the apartment and kept Jan's car in top shape, while Jan cooked most of the meals and did Brittany's hair for special events, since she never had time to get to a beauty shop herself.

They had been sharing an apartment in Seaview now for three years. It wasn't a big town by any means. Oddly, it wasn't by the sea either and the standard joke was that it was named in anticipation of "the big quake" that would show up one day, bringing the coast to them. A joke in poor taste, but if you lived in California, you either joked about earthquakes or you moved.

Seaview was one of the newer towns spread out inland away from the big cities, but within reasonable driving distance if you happened to work in the big city. The closest big one in their case was San Francisco. They were far enough away to not experience the chill weather and fogs off the bay. They enjoyed such mild weather, in fact, that Sunnyview would have been a much more appropriate name for them.

It was great having a roommate she got along so well with. Jan was petite, effervescent, always had a boyfriend on hand for anything she wanted to do, whether it was the same one or not, she didn't particularly care. She liked men, had a need to always have one around, even if she didn't take any of them seriously. Her only fault, if it could be termed one, was that she was a matchmaker at heart. She might not be able to settle on any one man in particular herself, but she saw no reason that her friends couldn't.

Brittany had proven to be a challenging subject for matchmaking though, and not for the usual reasons. She was beautiful, intelligent, responsible, had interesting careers, and admirable goals. She just happened to be six feet tall.

Height had always been a problem for Brittany, from childhood on. It put a serious restriction on the relationships she could develop, to the point where she had stopped putting any effort into developing one.

She had tried dating men shorter than her, but it never worked. The jokes would come out eventually about her height, or the man would get ribbed by his friends, or more often, their faces, would accidentally brush against her breasts— deliberately of course. She had decided when she did marry, her husband would have to at least be as tall as she was. Taller would be nice, but she wouldn't hold her breath on getting that lucky, would settle for the same height.

Yet such a problem did tend to make her notice tall men right off. Unfortunately, with a lot of really tall men, most of that height was naturally in their legs, and on some men, this tended to look a bit odd, particularly on the skinny ones. She'd take odd, though. She wasn't particular, just particular about not wanting to look down on her husband.

But a husband was a long way off for her, despite her age approaching thirty, or so she'd thought. Not that she hadn't wanted one eventually, but she was goal oriented, and she had one major goal that all her efforts were put into these days, owning her own home that she built with her own hands.

To that end, she worked two jobs, part-time at the local health spa in the evenings and all day on Saturdays, where she kept herself in good shape while doing the same for others, regulating diets and exercise programs. Her full-time job through the week was with Arbor Construction.

Sunday was her only day off, and the only chance she had to take care of the normal activities of life, like writing her family, balancing the checkbook, bill payments, house cleaning, laundry, shopping, repairing her car, etc. It was also the only day she had to simply relax, and preferred to spend that free time catching up on sleep or working on designing her dream house, not working on a relationship. The two jobs gave her next to no time for socializing, which was why she had stopped trying—until she met Thomas Johnson.

She had tried seeing the same man more than once, every Sunday actually, tried it with more than a few men thanks to her roommate's persistence. But that never worked out well, because they soon resented that she wasn't available more often. She'd been waiting until after she had her house. She could quit the second job, then have the same free-time that everyone else enjoyed. Then would be soon enough to start looking for a serious relationship.

Tom had changed her mind about that. She had begun to think she'd never find the right man for her, but Thomas Johnson filled the bill beyond her expectations. He was six foot six so he met her major criteria, but he was also exceptionally handsome and an established executive in advertising. She was blue-collar, he was white, but they still found common ground. He might make her feel self-conscious occasionally, but that was too minor a thing to counter her belief that he was the one for her. Stubborn certainty might better describe it, but then she *was* Irish.

Actually, her last name might give testament to that, but her family were Americans to the core. Her grandfather Callaghan had owned a farm in Kansas that he built from scratch and that her father inherited when he died. This is where she and her three brothers grew up. None of the Irish part of their history had been preserved, if anything was known about it, because her grandfather had been orphaned too young to have learned any of it.

But their first names, well, it wasn't hard to guess that her parents had been a bit flaky when they'd started having children. They denied being part of the hippy generation, called themselves "free-spirited," whatever that meant, and in fact, they had met while hiking across country, and had gone off to see the world together. They were hitch-hiking through England when the first child came along, and had been so impressed with that country, that their sons got named York, Kent, and Devon, in that order.

As the only girl who showed up last, Brittany got named after the entire country. Her parents took offense when it was pointed out that Brittany was actually a province in France, and not the shortened version of Great Britain.

Brittany had a no-nonsense attitude about life. You lived it, and eventually, you might even enjoy living it. That was actually a joke or meant to be, yet it wasn't that far off the mark on her own life. She actually liked her jobs, got a lot of satisfaction out of them, she just missed having the time to do all the little things in life that everyone else took for granted. But then she was no stranger to hard work and having little time for simple pleasures. Growing up on a farm, you went to school, then came home to endless chores. She hadn't had much free time then, and when she left home, even less.

She had made time for Tom, though. They'd been dating for four months now, went out every Saturday night, spent every Sunday together. As a busy executive who often worked late into the evenings during the week, his time was also somewhat restricted, so he never complained that he couldn't see her more often, was probably relieved that she had no such complaints either. He hadn't mentioned marriage yet, but she didn't doubt that he would soon, and her answer was going to be yes. Which was why she had finally made the decision to give up her virginity to him.

It was an odd thing to still have at her age, odd enough that it caused a good deal of embarrassment if she was forced to own up to it. That usually only happened when whoever she'd been dating started putting the pressure on to have sex. But the result of her confession would always be the same, laughter on their part—or disbelief.

Tom didn't know. He merely thought she was being cautious. It was more than that. Heavy necking was fine, could be fun or incredibly frustrating, but going all the way required more than just liking, at least for her. She needed feelings first, strong feelings, and she had those now. . . .

"Tonight's the night then?" Jan said from the doorway of Brittany's bedroom with a knowing grin.

"Yes," Brittany replied and managed not to blush about it.

"Hot damn!"

Brittany rolled her eyes. "Let's not discuss it, or I'll get cold feet."

"Cold? It's a wonder your feet haven't moldered, you've waited so long—"

"Which part of 'not discuss it' did you misunderstand?" Brittany cut in.

"Okay, okay," Jan conceded with a chuckle. "Just trying to alleviate some of that nervousness you're drowning in. You've been tense about this all day, when there's no need. You *are* sure about him, aren't you?"

"Yes, I—" Brittany started, then groaned. "Oh, God, you're going to make me have second thoughts!"

"Don't do that! Okay, I'm shutting up. Zipped lips. You're going to have a great time tonight. Stop worrying. This guy's right for you. Hell, he'd be right for anyone! He's almost too perfect to be believed—no, scratch that. I didn't say that. Didn't I say I was shutting up?"

Brittany smiled, grateful for Jan's silliness. She *had* been tense, when she shouldn't be. She'd made the decision, had been agonizing over it for weeks, but was satisfied that it was the right step for her at this point. She *was* sure about Tom. That was all that really mattered—wasn't it?

America Loves Lindsey!
The Timeless Romances of
The New York Times Bestselling Author

Johanna Lindsey

NEW YORK TIMES BESTSELLER

HOME FOR *the* HOLIDAYS

From America's #1 Bestselling Author

JOHANNA LINDSEY

An enchanting tale of two warring hearts warmed
and delightfully joined in a season of giving.

Available in a large print edition from HarperLargePrint

0-06-019909-1

Available wherever books are sold,
or call 1-800-331-3761 to order.

HarperCollins*Publishers*
www.harpercollins.com

HHL 1101